Someone has removed Judy Myers' headstone from the graveyard. Someone has left a freshly killed dog in the old Myers house. Someone has broken into a store and stolen a Halloween mask and several long knives.

SOMEONE HAS RETURNED TO HADDON-FIELD AFTER 15 BITTER YEARS OF EXILE . . . SOMEONE WHO WILL STRIKE AGAIN . . . AND AGAIN . . . AND AGAIN . . .

MOUSTAPHA AKKAD
presents

DONALD PLEASENCE
in
JOHN CARPENTER'S

Halloween

with
JAMIE LEE CURTIS   P. J. SOLES
NANCY LOOMIS

Written by
JOHN CARPENTER and DEBRA HILL

Executive producer
IRWIN YABLANS

Directed by
JOHN CARPENTER

Produced by
DEBRA HILL

From an original idea by
IRWIN YABLANS

Panavision   Metrocolor
A Compass International Pictures Release

Halloween

A Novel
by
Curtis Richards

Based on the Screenplay
by John Carpenter and Debra Hill

BANTAM BOOKS
TORONTO · NEW YORK · LONDON

HALLOWEEN
*A Bantam Book / published by arrangement with
Compass International*

Bantam edition / October 1979
2nd printing
3rd printing
4th printing
5th printing

ISBN 0–553–13226–1

Published simultaneously in the United States and Canada

---

*Bantam Books are published by Bantam Books, Inc. Its trade-
mark, consisting of the words "Bantam Books" and the por-
trayal of a bantam, is Registered in U.S. Patent and Trademark
Office and in other countries. Marca Registrada. Bantam
Books, Inc., 666 Fifth Avenue, New York, New York 10019.*

PRINTED IN THE UNITED STATES OF AMERICA

For Ronnie—Trick or Treat

Halloween

Prologue

The horror started on the eve of Samhain, in a foggy vale in northern Ireland at the dawn of the Celtic race. And once started, it trod the earth forevermore, wreaking its savagery suddenly, swiftly, and with incredible ferocity. Then, its lust sated, it shrank back into the mists of time for a year, a decade, a generation perhaps. But it slept only and did not die, for it could not be killed. And on the eve before Samhain it would stir, and if the lust were powerful enough, it would rise to fulfill the curse invoked so many Samhains before. Then the people would bolt their doors.

Scant good it did them, for the thing laughed at locks and bolts, and besides, there were the unwary. Always the unwary.

Samhain. The Druid festival of the dead. The summer had passed, and so too had that outburst of early fall warmth now known as Indian summer. The green had gone out of the land, the crops harvested, and the chill of winter had descended like an angel of death. The people, fearing the sun might never again warm the land, held their festival to appease Muck Olla, their deity. On hillsides and in the caves and daub-and-wattle huts great fires were lit to which the spirits of the departed were invited by their kinsmen to warm themselves, to be cheerful before the

1

snows blanketed the earth. Druid priests divined who would live and die in the coming year, who would marry, bear children, wax rich, enjoy good health. And they attempted to hold at bay, through sacrifices and other rites, the witches and goblins that ran amok at that time, stealing infants, destroying crops, killing farm animals ... and sometimes worse.

Deirdre was the third and youngest daughter of the Druid king Gwynwyll. Her hair was sandy brown with amber highlights, her eyes sea green, her complexion cream and wild rose. She was already taller than her older sisters, and her early development had been the cause of much concern in the tribal community. The other virgins tittered with envy; the married women voiced disapproval and counseled her mother to marry her off before the girl yielded to her budding impulses; the young warriors eyed her yearningly, and the old warriors thought forbidden thoughts and reflected on their faded memories.

His name was Enda. He was fifteen, and he loved Deirdre with a secret passion that tortured him and at night caused him to cry out in his sleep. When it became rumored that Deirdre's father, the king, was preparing to offer her hand in marriage, Enda consulted his kinsmen and asked if they thought his suit would be looked upon with favor. He suspected what the answer would be, but his longing overcame his embarrassment.

"Ho! Deirdre marry you?" his father cackled. "With your shriveled arm and your twitching mouth?" For Enda had presented himself wrong end first when his mother birthed him, and the midwives had made a botch of his delivery.

"She would as soon marry my goat!" howled his uncle.

"Or Bulech!" his brother added, pointing to

the runty dog worrying a greasy bone in the corner of their hut.

"Besides," said his father, "I'm told she's all but betrothed to Cullain."

"Now *there's* a lad worthy of that wench's pretty hole!" his uncle burst out, raising his wineskin to his fat lips, and they continued to discuss Deirdre's charms as Enda retreated miserably from the hut into the cold night.

The boy suffered tortures such as only the adolescent can. At length, he determined on a plan. If he could somehow get directly to Deirdre, he would convince her that though he was ill-favored physically, he was in every other respect a fitting candidate for her hand. This was easier said than done, however, because the virgins were closely watched by their mothers or by truculent warrior brothers. Nevertheless, one day Enda seized an opportunity when Deirdre went to fetch water from the stream at the foot of the hill. He followed her furtively, darting from tree to tree until he found her stooped over the stream, singing softly to herself as the water filled her clay pitchers.

"Deirdre?" he called timidly.

She turned and gasped, eyes round with fright.

"You! What do you want?" Her body tensed, and she seemed ready to bolt.

"I . . . I want to . . ." The panic in her face alarmed him. He had expected to startle her, but had not imagined she would greet him with such revulsion. He stepped forward, hand extended pacifically. But she jumped back, misinterpreting the gesture. She stumbled, almost falling into the stream, and Enda moved swiftly to rescue her.

"No!" she shrieked. "Get away from me, monster!" She found her feet and burst into a run, crying, "Help! Help! He means to rape me!"

Enda's body had been deformed at birth, but not until that moment had his soul been deformed . . .

And now it was Samhain, and Enda, humiliated beyond reason, stood on the perimeter of the celebrants dancing and chanting around the bonfire. In his left hand he held a fat wineskin, from which he drank often. In his right he held a footlong butcher blade which he used to cut the throats of pigs and chickens.

His eyes were fixed bitterly on the figures of Deirdre and Cullain, whirling exuberantly around the fire, to the immense approval of the tribe. For their betrothal had been announced, to the joy and relief of all.

Enda's legs shook and his body trembled in the cold night, though the heat of the fire was intense. And when the couple pirouetted past him once more, he leapt like a wildcat on his twin prey. Unarmed, their elbows linked, they didn't have a chance. Enda's blade sliced easily through Cullain's jugular and windpipe. His legs kicked out in a grotesque finale to his dance of life. Then he fell like a slaughtered bull, dragging Deirdre downward. Her head turned away, she laughed, believing that her drunken partner had merely stumbled. Enda's blade caught her with laughter on her face, the same laughter that had mocked him after she had run safely into the arms of her tribesmen the day he had approached her at the stream. The highly honed weapon plunged into her breast up to the hilt. In the clamor, no one heard the expulsion of wind from her lungs, the gurgle of blood, the whimper, or saw the look of dreadful recognition as the light faded from her eyes—except for Enda.

The thrill of revenge was the last emotion Enda knew, for a moment later he was literally torn apart by the enraged tribe. Only his head and his heart were preserved, gathered up after the frenzy had subsided, at the request of the grieving king. After Deirdre and Cullain were buried on the hallowed ground the following day, Enda's head and heart were carried to the summit of the Hill of Fiends, where cowards and other outcasts were left to rot unblessed. The king asked his shaman to pronounce a special curse over the remains of this vile murderer. "Thy soul shall roam the earth till the end of time, reliving thy foul deed and thy foul punishment, and may the god Muck Olla visit every affliction upon thy spirit forevermore."

The sky darkened and lightning flashed. The day suddenly grew black and cold, and out of nowhere gusts of snow lashed the tribal party. In the history of the tribe, it had never snowed so early in the year. Satisfied that Muck Olla had heard his prayer, the shaman summoned his people to turn their backs on Enda and return to their bereft village . . .

The celebration of Samhain's eve was transmuted over the centuries. The invading Romans carried the tradition back from the English Isles with them in the form of the Harvest Festival of Pomona, and the early Christians deemed their celebration Hallowmas. The popes of the Middle Ages consecrated November 1 as All Saints' Day, and All Hallow Even slurred into Halloween as the holiday was transmuted over the next millennium.

With the coming of modern civilization, the superstitions and traditions of the original festival lost their meaning and vitality. Token recognition could be seen in the custom of lighting candles in jack-o'-lanterns, hanging effigies of witches and goblins outside homes, and playing good-natured pranks that were a feeble cry from the mayhem of the old times. Children paraded about in costumes whose significance had long ago lost their correspondence to the terror of evil that had once gripped the world at the onset of winter. Halloween, like many of the holidays, had become an empty sham.

Except that from time to time, the innocent frolic of All Hallow Even was shattered by some brutal and inexplicable crime, and the original spirit of the celebration was brought home to a horrified world. Then the people would bolt their doors.

Scant good it did them . . . and besides, there were always the unwary.

1

It was 1963, and America was sure of itself, or at least seemed to be. Particularly in Haddonfield, Illinois. The tensions of the Cold War, of Cuba, the dark stirrings in Southeast Asia, lapped at the door of this placid and undistinguished midwestern town, but didn't really touch it. In less than a month, the president would be murdered in Dallas, signaling an era of tremendous violence and heartbreak that would reach deeply into the homes and hearts of Americans across the land.

But that was in the future, and tonight, October 31, was a time for fun. It was Halloween. Perhaps even more than Christmas, it was the most innocent holiday on the calendar. Yes, more than Christmas, because Christmas celebrated a happy event, and jolly St. Nick was a benevolent symbol anyway. But Halloween's origins were darker, very much darker, and if the children celebrated it as a happy event like Christmas, it was a symptom of how far we'd come from the time when mankind respected the forces of evil.

Little Michael Myers's grandmother clucked her disapproval as the visiting rosy-faced six-year-old showed her the costume in the Woolworth box. "What's that supposed to be?" she said, leaning forward in her recliner and adjusting her specs.

"A clown, Grandma." He ran his hand over

7

the red and green nylon jester's costume, with matching cap with a pompom on top.

"A clown," she sighed.

"Now, Mother," Michael's mother, Edith, came to the rescue, "I know what you're going to say."

"Well, it's true, darn it. We never had that five-and-dime junk when we grew up on the farm. We took Halloween seriously. Why, when we set up scarecrows and jack-o'-lanterns, it was because we were genuinely trying to scare off the bogeyman. Bogeyman, now he played *real* pranks and did some *real* damage. He didn't just go around like they do today, slapping people's clothes with socks filled with chalk-dust and soaping their windows."

"What did the bogeyman do, Grandma?"

Mrs. Myers shifted uncomfortably in her chair. "I don't think Michael wants to hear that," she said, looking significantly at her mother. "It might give him bad dreams."

But grandma wasn't taking the warning. "Nothing wrong with bad dreams. At least they remind us that things aren't hunky-dory in this world. Lord, everything is so clean and—*phony* these days. Just one big television commercial. Clown costumes!" she sighed, fingering the cheap material in the Woolworth box.

"What did the bogeyman *do?*" Michael insisted.

The silver-haired woman leaned forward confidentially, a perverse smile lighting her pleasantly lined face. "Well, if you were lucky, you got away with nothing worse than finding some of your chickens beheaded."

"Beheaded?"

"Their heads cut off," she explained with a relish. Michael's eyes widened; his mother grimaced and picked up a copy of *Look*, riffling ner-

vously through it. "If you weren't so lucky, you
lost a cow or two."

"Unheaded?"

"*Be*-headed, yes."

"Were the heads just lying there next to the
cows or were they . . . ?"

"Mother, that will be enough. Really!" Mrs.
Myers gasped, snapping the magazine shut.

But grandma had warmed to the subject.
Behind her spectacles, her blue eyes had drifted
off to her girlhood, and her head nodded in memory of some awesome event. "Once he burned
somebody's barn down. Was it Winfield? No, *Winter*field. Burned Mr. Winterfield's barn down to
the ground, livestock and all." She looked at the
wide-eyed boy, then at her horrified daughter,
and realized she'd gone too far. "Of course, Michael, we always suspected it wasn't the Bogeyman. Perhaps neighbors getting even with each
other for some slight. In costumes and masks, it
was easier to get away with that sort of thing. But
I do remember one incident . . ."

"Not the chimney story," begged Mrs. Myers.

"Oh, tell me the chimney story!" implored
the grandson.

"Well," the woman said, taking her grandson
up on her lap, "it was Halloween, nineteen-ought
. . . nine? Nineteen ten?"

"Just tell it," said Michael. Even at six he
recognized a boring attack of grandma's What-
year-was-it-again?

"Yes. It was Halloween, but way after mid-
night. Maybe two or three in the morning. We'd
all gone to sleep, leaving the fire burning in the
parlor because it was a terribly cold night. Well,
suddenly I hear my brother Jimmy shouting,
'Smoke! Smoke! Wake up everybody, the house is
on fire!' I grabbed my robe and rushed down the
stairs right behind my daddy, who'd picked up the

bucket of water we always kept filled at the top of the landing. Sure enough, the whole downstairs was thick with woodsmoke. But I couldn't see any fire. The smoke was coming from the fireplace, and it looked as though the flue had been closed."

"What's a flue?"

Grandma explained what a flue was. "We put out the embers and opened the doors and windows to let the smoke out. Then daddy looked at the flue and—glory be—it was open. Something was jamming up the chimney. Now, we didn't have a ladder on account of daddy having just taken it apart to replace some rotten rungs. So Jimmy had to shinny himself up the drainpipe to find out what was obstructing the chimney."

"What was it?" the boy asked, while his mother shook her head in painful anticipation.

"A dead hog."

"Wow!"

"Someone—or something—had cut our hog's throat and laid it atop the chimney." She laughed humorlessly. "The thing is, that hog weighed near three hundred pounds. How did it get up there without a ladder? Without our hearing anything? Without our dog, Toby, raising hob with his barking like he usually did when he heard something prowling? Without disturbing a gate or making a footprint? Answer me that, Mister Woolworth Clown Costume."

"I don't know."

"Well, I do. 'Twas the bogeyman, that's all there is to it."

"Mother, that will do!" Mrs. Myers snapped. "The boy's been having problems enough at night without your adding to them."

"Problems? What kind . . . ? Um, Michael honey, run into the bedroom and try the costume on for Grandma. I'll tuck it if it's too baggy."

"It's supposed to be baggy," said the little boy, carrying the box into the next room.

"Now, what's this about 'problems'?" she demanded of her daughter.

Edith Myers, a younger, darker-eyed replica of her mother, ran a hand through her curly blond hair. "I told you, he's been getting into fights at school. At home, too, with Judith. He's been wetting his bed again, which he hasn't done in three years."

"Fighting about what?"

"Mother, can we just forget . . . ?"

The old woman's eyes narrowed. "No, we can't. What kind of trouble is that boy in?"

"Voices," Mrs. Myers finally blurted after a minute's tortured pause. "He hears voices."

"Oh, Little Lord Jesus!" the old woman cried. She exchanged a long, meaningful look with her daughter. "I'm afraid to ask what these voices say."

" 'They tell me to say I hate people.' That's how Michael put it when I asked him. Don thinks maybe we ought to send Michael to someone."

"You mean a psychiatrist?"

"Yes."

"I don't put much stock in psychiatrists, but I don't suppose it could hurt. And I don't think it will help, if it's what I'm thinking."

The younger woman began to get agitated. "I know what you're thinking, and that's why I didn't want to get into this with you. You're going to say that that's how it started with Grandpa Nordstrom."

"We have to face up to it, child, that *is* how it started with your father's father."

"Mother, all children hear imaginary voices. Don't you remember my Bobby Bear, who used to . . . ?"

"It's not the same. At least, it's not something you should ignore. Does the boy have dreams?" Her daughter nodded. "Does he remember any?"

"Yes, and they're very violent." Her face reddened and she turned her eyes away from her mother's piercing gaze. "Mother, when Grandpa Nordstrom . . . that is . . . Well, you've never spoken to us about that incident, and I think there are enough similarities . . ."

"Hush, here comes Michael. When you get home, call me as soon as you can, I think the time has come to tell you everything. Ah, there's my little boy," she cooed as Michael came back into the room with a rustle, "right out of a Punch 'n' Judy show."

He stood before them, an angel in red and green nylon, elastic ankle- and wrist-bands making the costume cling at the extremities and bag out everywhere else. A ruff around the neck and the little droopy pompom cap completed the charming picture.

"Grandma's baby!" she laughed, clasping the boy to her bosom. "Edith, please fetch me some cold cream and lipstick from the tray in my bedroom. Might as well complete the picture."

"I don't want makeup," Michael protested.

"Of course you do. You don't want anyone to guess who you are when you go around playing pranks."

"I'm not going to play pranks. I'm just going to ask for candy."

"You do that, child. You just have an innocent, Woolworth kind of Halloween."

She saw them out the door. "Remember, Edith, call me soon as you can."

"I will, Mother. And don't worry."

"I won't," she said, shutting the door. She began to tremble, wondering if she should have said something to her daughter about Grandpa Nordstrom's dreams.

2

Judy Myers, nude except for a pair of panties with red valentines printed on them, sat before her mirror brushing her long blond hair. She sang to herself, stressing each third note as she pulled the tortoise-shell brush downwards to her shoulders. She liked gazing at herself, noting how her breasts flattened when she brought the brush to her head, then rounded and filled again when the brush reached the bottom of its stroke. She was especially happy this evening because the house was empty, a rare occasion indeed.

The house being empty meant no parents to bug her, no kid brother to burst in on her or try to pinch her boobs or ass, or maybe peek at her through the keyhole. More importantly, it meant that she could make out with Danny on a couch or maybe even in bed without having to worry about interruptions. Fooling around in cars wasn't terribly satisfying anymore. Now that it was getting cold, you had to roll up the windows and keep the heater on and it got stuffy and steamy. And now that she and Danny had gone all the way, she was eager to do it with him in a civilized fashion. Danny's suggestion of a motel in Mapleton was not what she meant by civilized fashion.

The doorbell rang.

"Oh, God, he's here already!" she muttered, snatching up her unsexy bulky chenille robe and

13

stepping into fuzzy slippers. She looked at the
alarm clock on the night table. It was a quarter to
seven. Danny was fifteen minutes early. "I'll kill
him. Look at me. Yuchh."

The doorbell went off again, long and insis-
tent. "Yeah, I'm coming, I'm coming!" Though
she knew she'd end up undressed anyway, she'd
at least wanted to start out clothed for Danny,
and clothed in a halfway decent way, for crying
out loud, and not like some frumpy washerwoman.
She galumphed down the stairs, getting really
pissed off, and flung open the door. "Goddamn it,
Danny, you told me . . ."

"Trick or treat!"

There were eight of them, holding shopping
bags. A few also held UNICEF boxes with slots
in them for coins to give to their class charity.
Their uniforms were all cheap and store-bought
except for one girl tricked out in her mother's
peasant skirt and blouse and a gypsy shawl. There
was a pirate, a cowboy, a ballerina, two Wonder
Women in identical five-and-dime outfits, the
gypsy girl, a space man, and a clown. The costumes were chintzy and looked as if they'd tear if
you stuck your tongue out at them. They all wore
masks, but Judy identified most of them. The
space man and cowboy were Adam and Charlie
Becket, the pirate and ballerina were Chris and
Hope Ritzinger. The gypsy was Katie Schaller.
One Wonder Woman looked like Christine Frank,
but Judy couldn't figure out who the other was.

And of course, she guessed who the clown
was, as she'd put the finishing touches on his
outfit herself.

"Trick or treat!" they repeated.

"Oh yeah?" Judy teased. "And what if I
don't give you any treat?

The children stood silently, puzzled. No one
had ever denied them. They just assumed you
filled their bags with goodies. If you turned them

down, they wouldn't know what tricks to play.
Judy stood in the doorway enjoying their discomfort for a moment. To her right, on a little table
in the hall, were six bowls filled with candy corn,
Tootsie Rolls, Baby Ruths, Good 'n' Plenty, popcorn, and Hershey Kisses. There was also a dish
with pennies in it for the UNICEF collection.

"Huh? What are you gonna do if I don't give
you anything?"

They shrugged, shuffled their feet, giggled
nervously.

Then one of them said, "We're gonna kill
you."

Judy sucked in her breath. "Who said that?"

The children looked at each other, then looked
back at her.

"Michael Myers, was that you? Because if it
was, it's not funny, and I'm telling mother and
father when they come home."

"I'm not Michael Myers, I'm a clown."

Judy caught the glint of Danny's '59 Chevy
turning into the street. "Okay, kids, you win.
Hold out your bags." She stepped to the bowls and
grabbed handfuls of candy, showering it into each
bag. Then she took up the dish of pennies and
dropped four or five into each of the contribution
boxes.

"Thank you," they said politely. "Good-bye.
Happy Halloween," they shouted over their shoulders as they toddled off to their next house.

Judy closed the door and bolted up the stairs
two at a time, stripping out of her robe as she
did. When she reached the top of the landing she
kicked off her fuzzies and threw the robe into her
closet, grabbing a blouse and skirt, rummaging
through her drawers for a bra and a pair of knee-
socks and a sweater. She donned these in record
time, and when the doorbell rang she was ready
in a demure collegiate-looking outfit. Although
both she and Danny knew where they were going

to end up tonight, she decided she should at least *look* a little hard to get, otherwise Danny would think she was fast, and that would get around school.

She caught her breath, then descended the stairs in stately steps. She opened the door calmly, as if she'd almost forgotten they had a date.

"Oh, Danny, it's you."

The tall, muscular boy cocked his head. "Of course it's me. Who'd you expect, Seth Dooley?" Dooley was the class goof and the last person Judy would ever date.

"No, I thought it was some more kids trick-or-treating. Come in."

He entered and shut the door behind him. "I thought we'd do a little trick-or-treating of our own," he said, putting his arms around her. "First you give me some of those Hershey Kisses, then I play with your Tootsie Rolls, then we have some Good 'n' Plenty. Yummm." He buried his lips in the nape of her neck.

Judy giggled, then squirmed out of his grasp. "That's what you think. Look at you. You dress in jeans and a polo shirt and you expect a girl to strip off her clothes?"

He laughed. "What does it matter what we have on? It's what we're going to have off that counts." He lunged for her again but she ducked out of his grasp.

"Not so fast, buster. First of all, it's not even dark yet. Second of all, I'm worried that more kids are going to come around and interrupt us while we're . . . uh, discussing homework. And third of all, I don't even know if I feel like doing anything. You take a lot for granted, you know."

"Yeah, I'm a real animal," he said, pretending to smack himself on the wrist.

"Besides, my mother and father'll be home any second," she said, flouncing away into the kitchen.

He followed close on her heels. "The hell they will be. You told me they always go to the movies on Halloween because they hate the doorbell ringing. Hey, what are you doing with that knife?"

From the drawer under the sink, Judy had removed a long carving knife and now held it menacingly above her head. "I'm going to cut off your whatsamajiggy, that's what I'm going to do," she hissed like a witch.

"Hey, come on now," Danny said, backing away toward the kitchen counter, "that's not funny. You could hurt someone with that thing."

"That's the whole idea, my pretty," she said, sounding a little like the Wicked Witch of the West. She rushed at him, and he jumped out of the way as the blade plunged to the hilt into . . .

. . . a fat pumpkin.

Judy laughed. "You goof. I'm just making a jack-o'-lantern."

Danny stood plastered against the far wall of the kitchen, panting. "Oh, that's funny. That's terribly funny. Some sense of humor you have. Ha ha ha. You could have *killed* someone, for crying out loud."

"Just help me cut the cap off this thing, will you? The sooner you do, the sooner we can do our homework."

Danny caught his breath, then relieved her of the treacherous eight-inch blade and began carefully sawing around the top of the pumpkin until the crown came off. He set this aside, then called for a large cooking spoon and began scooping the seeds and stringy pulp out of the shell. "Looks like he has more brains than you do."

"Shut up and finish the job," she said, curling her arms around him from behind. "I'm getting hungry, and it's not for pumpkin seeds."

Her hands slid down his chest and belly, and Danny's knees went weak. Then he took up the knife again and sliced into the side of the pumpkin. "Baby, I'm going to set a new speed record for pumpkin cutting." Deftly he cut out two triangular eyes and a triangular nose, then a long, wide mouth with jagged teeth. "Got a candle?"

"What for?" Her eyes sparkled with mischief.

"For the pumpkin, stupid." He gazed unbelievingly at her, then said, "Oh, I get it." He shook his head. "I sometimes wonder if women don't have dirtier minds than men."

"Lucky for you they do," she said, producing a stubby candle from the pantry.

He cut a socket in the base of the pumpkin, lit the candle and set in inside. Then he bored a few little air holes in the cap with a smaller knife to allow the flame oxygen.

They cleaned up and Judy put the cutlery away while Danny carried the jack-o'-lantern out to the front porch of the white clapboard house. It glowed intensely in the cool autumn air, projecting its grotesque smile to the dozens of other jack-o'-lanterns that lined the placid street. Danny was not a particularly intellectual boy, but for a moment he looked out at the row of shimmering orange pumpkin-faces and wondered what dark forces these totems were once intended to repel.

The night was quiet and starry, with a slight breeze starting up from the north—good football weather, Danny reflected. From somewhere down the street came the dim echo of "Trick or treat!" shouted by a roving band of children. For the first time Danny wondered about all these traditions—jack-o'-lanterns, paper witches and cardboard skeletons, trick-or-treating, apple-dunking, ghosts and goblins. But he didn't wonder long. He was getting cold.

And horny.

Judy was just finishing sponging up the orange pumpkin juice from the kitchen counter.

She dried her hands on a paper towel, then turned to find Danny.

"*Boo!*"

Judy's heart almost pounded out of her chest. "God almighty, you scared the wits out of me!" she gasped, collapsing into Danny's arms. He'd donned a rubber fright-mask, a Frankenstein face with sunken eyes and a livid scar across the cheek.

He held her tightly, feeling her breasts heaving with fright through her sweater. He dug his fingers under the sweater and pulled her blouse-tail out of her skirt, then clamped his hands over the warm flesh of her back. She murmured and responded eagerly with her pelvis. He found the hook-and-eye of her bra straps and, after a brief fumble or two, managed to unfasten them and run his hands forward until they cupped her breasts. It always amazed him that she looked so modestly endowed underneath her clothing, yet when stripped she possessed a wonderful pair of breasts. She moaned as his palms and fingers enclosed them. Her nipples went from soft to hard almost instantly as his fingertips massaged and lightly pinched them.

"Kiss them," she begged.

"Are you sure?" came his hollow voice.

She took her head off his chest and burst into laughter. He still had his Frankenstein mask on.

"Take that thing off."

"You take your thing off, and I'll take my thing off."

"It's a deal."

He stripped off the mask and took her by the hand to the foot of the stairs. "Are you sure about your parents?"

"They won't be back till ten at least."

"And Michael?"

"I told you, he's trick-or-treating. We have time, but not all night, so no more yakking, huh?"

"No more yakking."

She turned her back on him and sauntered up the stairs, wiggling her behind enticingly and stripping out of her sweater and blouse before she'd reached the landing. Danny followed like a hungry puppy, tossing his own clothes off as he went along.

Stripped of all but her panties, she stood before him in the dim light of the night table lamp. Her breasts rose and fell excitedly, her red nipples poking provocatively through the blond tresses that cascaded over them.

Danny stared incredulously. He'd never seen anything so beautiful. Up to now his knowledge of his girl had been restricted to his Braille reading of her body in dark cramped automobiles, but now he feasted on her exquisite firmness, almost forgetting to take his own pants off.

At last he unbuckled his belt and pulled his jeans and shorts to his ankles simultaneously. He was already erect.

"Oh," Judy murmured, eyes widening.

He stepped up to her and embraced her, his hands enclosing her buttocks. She lowered herself on the bed, parted her thighs wide, and admitted him. Slowly, joyously, he entered her. "Oh," she murmured again. She put her hands on his buttocks and pulled him into her with feline ferocity, exulting in the powerful muscles that filled her body and soul with ecstasy.

"So this is what it's like to do it in a bed," she whispered.

"This is what it's like to do it in a bed."

3

He stood in the shadow of the tall hedgerow, looking and listening. He had seen them necking in the kitchen, then Danny had come out on the porch for a minute to set the jack-o'-lantern down. When Danny returned, they had gone upstairs. A few minutes later, the light in Judy's bedroom had gone off. Now, above the rustle of the wind in the crisp leaves of the huge oaks on the front lawn, he could hear their sighs, moans, and giggles.

And they filled him with murderous hatred.

The voice in his head had become subdued for the moment as he listened to Judy and Danny, not really understanding the significance of their utterances except that it had to do with love. He had heard similar sounds coming from his mother and father's room. But he had felt warmly toward them. They were making each other happy, his father and mother, and that made him happy too.

Then why did he feel such poisonous rage against his sister and her boyfriend?

It was the voice. The voice stirred up the hatred. It had done so in his dreams, and now it was doing so in real life. It had begun with the strange pictures in his head at night, pictures of people he had never seen—oh, maybe in comic books or on television, but never in real life. People in strange costumes, animal skins, armor,

21

leather, drinking and dancing wildly around a
fire. One couple in particular. They looked like
Judy and Danny, madly in love with each other,
dancing in a circle around the huge bonfire, while
he, Michael, stood in the crowd hating them, burning up with jealousy.

Then a voice had come into his head while he
dreamt, a voice telling him to stop the dancing
lovers. The voice had become louder, clearer, and
more demanding lately, and its dictates more com-
pelling. He had begun to believe that if he listened to the voice, did what it told him to do,
maybe the voice would go away and leave him
alone. It was no longer a dream voice. It spoke to
him during the waking time too. It had spoken
loudly to him tonight, even as he went from house
to house begging candy, even as he played games
at the party. It had directed him to return home
at once.

Looking around to make certain he wasn't
being observed, he slipped across the lawn past
the front porch, ducking stealthily to avoid the
orange glare of the jack-o'-lantern. He sidled
along the shingles on the side of the house and
tiptoed up the stairs of the side door. He turned
the knob and the door opened. He wasn't surprised. People didn't lock their doors in Haddonfield; what was there to fear?

He slipped into the kitchen and crossed to the
sink. *Go ahead,* the voice told him, *you know what
to do*. He opened the drawer and reached in. His
fingers enclosed the thing he was looking for, and
he withdrew it from the drawer.

It was the butcher knife.

He touched the tip with the meat of his index finger. It pricked him. He ran his thumb along
the edge of the eight-inch blade. It left a thin neat
trail of blood.

He glided out of the kitchen and into the parlor, where he paused, listening. He heard them

talking while they dressed and straightened up. He pressed himself against the wall as footsteps creaked down the stairs.

First he saw Danny, in jeans and blue-striped polo shirt. His hair was mussed and his cheeks were flushed as if he'd been kissed with hard passion. Then Judy, a sheet wrapped around her, which she held with her thumb against the base of her spine. The intruder gazed at her bare, dimpled buttocks and slender legs, then he fingered the blade of his knife, trembling.

They were kissing, and at last she let go of the sheet, so that all that held it up was the pressure of his body against hers. "Do you have to go?"

He held his watch up behind her head. "I gotta. Your folks'll be home any second."

She ran her hand up his thigh. "How about a quick one?"

"Here? Now? Are you crazy?"

"You are such a chicken."

"I'd be roast chicken if your parents discovered us doing it in the hall as they walked in the door." He pushed her away and the sheet fell to the floor. His eyes bulged as he took her body in one last time. "Jeez, it's tempting . . . No. No, I gotta go." He picked the sheet up and wrapped it around her once again. "See, chivalry is not dead."

"Too bad. Will you call me tomorrow?"

"Yeah, sure."

"Promise?"

"I'd have to be crazy not to, wouldn't I?"

They kissed one last time and parted like Romeo leaving Juliet. Judy shut the door behind him, leaned against it for a moment, and moaned in remembrance of recent ecstasies. Then she trotted back up the stairs.

He stepped out of the shadows of the parlor and furtively made his way up the stairs, pausing at the landing to look and listen. Her clothes were still strewn in a trail from the top of the stairs to her bed. He followed them like a hunter tracking the spoor of his prey. He stopped outside her open door, peering inside. She sat in her red valentine bikini panties, brushing her hair before the mirror on her dresser. She hummed a tune in her pretty voice.

He stepped into the room and was halfway across when she saw him. Her eyes clouded and her eyebrows knit with puzzlement. She crossed her wrists in front of her breasts. She recognized him through his mask and called his name, bewildered. "Michael, is this a joke . . . ?"

He continued coming at her.

"Get out of here, Goddamn it. Get out of here before I . . ."

The first slash of the knife caught her on the wrist, splashing blood across her chest and legs. She looked at the wound with more surprise than pain. She couldn't believe it was happening. Then she realized.

She jumped to her feet and backed away to the wall, knocking over her chair. "What are you doing? What are you doing?" she cried. As he raised the blade again, she held her hand out to protect herself. He slashed the hand viciously, and it dropped limply to her side. Now she was shrieking insanely as she grasped what was happening. He plunged the knife into her right breast, and a great gout of scarlet blood spurted out of the wound and soaked his hand and wrist. He thrust the blade into her belly. At what point she died, he didn't know, for now that she was defenseless he stuck the knife into her again and again, jamming it into her breasts, belly, groin, arms, legs, and throat. He stabbed her fifty times if he stabbed her once, exultation sweeping over him like no joy he had ever known.

The paroxysms began to die down and he

stood over her, spent. It was almost impossible to recognize this piece of hacked flesh. Blood was everywhere, and the sour odor of it rose up from his hands, intoxicating him.

The gory little figure turned and stepped over the fallen furniture and scattered clothing and walked down the stairs and into the kitchen. Suddenly he realized he was hungry. He reached into a bowl on the kitchen counter and stuffed a cookie into his mouth, then opened the refrigerator door and removed a bottle of milk. He emptied half of it into his mouth directly from the bottle and wiped his mouth with his bloody sleeve, leaving a streak of red and white across his cheek.

He opened the side door and went outside, still carrying the butcher knife. He stepped out onto the lawn and stood there for a minute indecisively.

At that moment a dark sedan pulled up to the curb. The assassin made no attempt to flee, but stood on the lawn waiting for the occupants of the car to get out. After a moment both front doors opened and a man and woman emerged. They took two or three paces toward the house, then saw him and stopped, staring at the figure in the bloodstained clown costume with a blood-clotted butcher knife in his hand.

The man reached out and removed the mask from the boy's face.

"Michael . . . ?"

4

They didn't know what to call him, and they didn't know what to do with him.

He wasn't a man, so he couldn't be tried for murder. He wasn't even an adolescent. And although the law respecting juveniles was broad enough to cover a six-year-old boy, it didn't seem appropriate that laws designed to handle vicious teenage punks, muggers, purse snatchers, and car thieves, should apply to him. To look at him, during the hearings before the magistrate, was to see a handsome, almost pretty, rosy-cheeked little lad in a neat tweed suit, a tie, and highly polished shoes. His eyes were warm, his smile genuine, and when he spoke it was with artless sincerity. In fact, more than one newspaper report described him as "charming."

Yet the boy had, by his own admission, stabbed his sister thirty-one times at least, the coroner testified. Probably more.

The magistrate concluded that the boy was either mad or lying. He questioned the little fellow very closely about whether some other person had done the deed and thrust the blade into the child's hand. But the boy's insistence on his story, and the absence of any other evidence—despite the fact that poor Danny, Judy's lover, was treated very roughly by police detectives, and came with-

in an ace of being accused—compelled the magistrate to declare it an act of madness.

Yet, knowing what sort of place the boy
would be sent to, and what sort of people he would
be thrown in with, the magistrate agonized over
the verdict that would deliver Michael into the
hands of those howling maniacs and their gang-
ster keepers that he had seen with his own eyes
on a recent official visit to the downstate center at
Smith's Grove.

Looking ashen and exhausted, he reconvened
the hearing a week later. "Ladies and gentlemen
of the court, in forty-two years as a loyal ser-
vant of the law and of this court, I have never
been asked to make as remotely cruel a decision
as the one I am now compelled to make. Even as I
speak I am aware that I'm struggling to keep my
eyes from gazing upon the accused in this bizarre
episode, for I know that if I do, I may falter in
my duty. Nevertheless, absent any evidence to the
contrary, absent any witnesses, absent any other
person to come forth with a confession, absent
any contradiction in the child's story, absent any
regret on the part of the accused, and above all,
absent any sense of right or wrong, which is the
foundation of the law with respect to the criminally insane—I have no choice but to remand
Michael Audrey Myers to the Smith's Grove Sanitarium in Warren County, Illinois, where he shall
be placed in the care of a resident psychiatrist
who shall report to this court regularly. His case
shall be reviewed no less than twice a year, and
upon recommendation of the psychiatrist the boy
may be released back into the custody of his parents.

"Although it is impossible for me to con-
ceive a lengthy stay for Michael, whose brutal
act I believe to have been the product of a passing
madness that I hope has discharged itself forever

from his system, I am obliged to cite the law concerning criminally insane minors, namely, that at the age of twenty-one they must be brought before a magistrate for a criminal proceeding.

"If Michael is still at Smith's Grove fifteen years hence, he shall be brought before the court on the day of his twenty-first birthday, where he shall be tried as an adult for the murder of Judith Margaret Myers.

"I have," he said, holding up a sheaf of papers, "prepared a list of supplementary instructions for the care of Michael at Smith's Grove, in the hope that the problems that exist in such institutions shall not damage his chances of returning to society as a normal, healthy, fully functional human being. This court is dismissed."

He rose, and the courtroom, which was composed almost exclusively of newspaper reporters, rose with him. He pivoted and, still averting his eyes from the boy he had just sentenced to the living death of an insane asylum, passed through the rear door of the courtroom. Michael's parents sobbed as the boy was led out of the room by a stern-looking matron, and even the normally tough-skinned reporters, who had seen everything, looked wan and reflective.

One observer, however, was unaffected. Sam Loomis, a round-faced man with a goatee and a head shaved bald, had been staring penetratingly at the accused boy. In all his years as a clinical psychiatrist, he had heard and read about such cases but had never observed one personally, and so the Myers case had interested him keenly— particularly because Loomis was the resident in charge of juveniles at Smith's Grove. Like everyone else, Loomis had been deeply touched by the angelic appearance and manner of the little boy until, as the boy was reciting the events of the evening of October 31, 1963, his eyes had happened to lock with Loomis's. The man felt a chilly forboding that almost curdled his blood . . .

Six months had passed since the hearing, and, as required by law, Loomis now appeared before Judge Christopher in the magistrate's chambers. As they sipped glasses of port, Loomis noted how much the judge seemed to have aged. Loomis tactfully said something to this effect.

"It disturbed me deeply then, and it disturbs me no less deeply now. It haunts my waking hours and my sleep. I don't think I've ever done anything so difficult in my life. But what could I have done? What would you have done? How is he?"

"He is . . . fine. Of course, in my professional capacity, 'fine' must be defined . . ."

"Please, no psychiatric rubbish, Loomis. Just tell me about his behavior in plain terms."

"In plain terms? He has done nothing, to our direct knowledge, that would indicate anything else but normality."

"*Direct* knowledge?"

"Judge Christopher," Loomis said, rising to his feet and distractedly running his fingers over the red and beige bound legal volumes on the judge's shelves, "there have been some peculiar and unpleasant occurrences at Smith's Grove in the last six months. Particularly in the juvenile ward."

The judge leaned forward. "Like what?"

"Well, first of all, you have to understand that as Michael is by far—maybe eight or nine years—the youngest patient in the ward, he would ordinarily be the subject of a great deal of bullying, yes?"

"I should imagine so."

"Well, there hasn't been any attempt whatsoever. Not so much as a pinch."

The magistrate stroked his cheek. "And what do you make of that?"

"The same thing you do, I'm sure. They're afraid of him. I have seen him turn the hardest delinquent in the ward to stone with a stare."

The judge digested it. "And this is all you have to say? You feel this is sufficient reason for me to extend his incarceration . . ."

"Then there was the matter of Gilden, the trustee. Gilden is known around the ward for his pranks. The children love him; he's the only breath of fresh air in the place. One day, about a month after Michael's arrival, old Gilden played one of his harmless practical jokes on the boy— one I've seen countless times."

"What was that?"

"Oh, he loosened the cap on the salt shaker, so that when Michael salted his dinner, the contents of the shaker fell into his food. As usual, it got a big laugh. It has become practically an initiation ceremony for the youngsters at the hospital."

"And . . . ?"

"Michael didn't think it was funny."

"What did he do?"

"Nothing, at the time. But that night, Gilden came down with a case of cramps so severe he had to have his stomach pumped. It was analyzed as food poisoning."

"But you think . . . ?"

"Yes, though I don't know how the boy might have gotten to the kitchen or what he could have used. The juvenile ward is separated from the kitchen by a series of guarded or locked passages."

"I see. Anything else?"

"Nothing quite as tangible. But the other boys in my charge have become . . . well, rather restless since Michael's arrival. Like a herd of cattle that instinctively feels the presence of wolves out there in the darkness. They always seem to be on the verge of bolting. Stampeding."

The judge looked at him. "Dr. Loomis, I think you know how profoundly unnerved this matter has made me, and how desperately interested I am in seeing Michael treated and released. I'm not overly impressed by the observations you've made this morning, and it's only your reputation that keeps me from making some rather critical remarks. Now, I want to know if the boy sticks to his story, understands what he did, feels remorseful, feels purged of the murderous hatred he described to us at the hearing, that sort of thing."

"Judge," said Loomis, collapsing into a leather chair, "the boy's story and attitude haven't changed a whit since the hearing, though I have spent nearly two hours a day with him every day for six months. I have nothing to go on but my experience and my hunches, and I tell you out of the depths of all I have learned and observed in fifteen years of exploration of the human mind, Michael Myers may be the most dangerous person I have ever handled."

Loomis's crystal blue eyes locked with Christopher's and held them for a long moment. Then the judge pulled his gaze away and quaffed down the rest of his port nervously. "Damn it, Loomis, I cannot run my court on hunches, hearsay, coincidences, or anything but hard evidence. So unless you can come up with *something*, something he says, something he does, I am going to seriously entertain the boy's release the next time you appear before me. Is that understood?"

"Yes, *Your Honor*," Loomis breathed, taking his leave with no ceremony whatever.

In the following months there were more "occurrences," and in Loomis's mind there was

no doubt whom to ascribe them to. Every time
Michael was slighted, or fancied he was, by a
staff member or another inmate, some awful vengeance was visited upon the offending person. It
might be a day, a week, a month later, but Michael
got even.

The problem for Loomis was that no one ever
observed the boy doing it directly. One day, as the
boys were watching television in the lounge, a
fifteen-year-old got up and turned the sound lower. Michael rose and turned it up again. The
other boy turned it lower again. Michael accepted
the situation with a resigned shrug.

That evening, as the older boy was showering, the water turned scalding. The lad was
harmed only enough to discomfort him for a
week, but it could have been serious, and everyone knew who was behind it. Yet apparently
Michael had not left his room.

There were other incidents. A nurse who
quarreled with Michael fell down the stairs two
days later, fracturing her pelvis. A boy who borrowed a game from Michael and forgot to return
it suffered a vicious rash that hospitalized him for
a month.

What doubly disturbed Loomis was that sub-
tly but definitely, the boy was capturing the lead-
ership of the juvenile ward, because no one dared
to challenge him. Everyone, staff and inmates
alike, indulged him, and so he pretty much got
his way.

Loomis wondered when his own turn would
come, but it never did, and he believed it was because no matter how much Loomis challenged the
boy, no matter how much he thwarted him, Michael knew that Loomis was trying to help him.
The boy grudgingly acknowledged Loomis's au-
thority, and that, Loomis concluded, was probably the only thing that prevented Michael from
walking scot-free out of the institution. "You could,

you know," Loomis said to him one afternoon
during their regular therapy session. "That's how
much they fear you. If you were to ask an orderly
for keys, ask a guard or trustee to turn his back at
the appropriate moment, you could stroll out of
here, such is the power you exert over them. Isn't
that true, Michael?"

The boy's eyes clouded and he shrugged
his shoulders. "I don't know what you mean,
sir."

"Ah, but you won't do it," Loomis said, almost smugly. "You won't do it because you have
it made here. Here you have your own little world.
If you were to escape, why, what would await
you out there but strife and hassle? So you stay
here, snug and secure, isn't that true, you little
dev——"

Loomis caught himself. No matter what he
believed, it was unprofessional to express it that
way, and besides, when you got right down to it,
*no one had ever seen the kid do anything to any-
body.*

Which is why, at this outburst of Loomis's
frustration, Michael simply fluttered his long eye-
lashes, smiled, and said, "I don't understand, Dr.
Loomis."

Loomis dreaded his next six-month review of
Michael's case with Judge Christopher, because
if Loomis couldn't produce any hard evidence of
wrongdoing on Michael's part, the judge might
very well order his release.

So it went, through the summer and early
fall. Then, one day in mid-October, at the end of
another fruitless therapy session, Michael dropped
a bomb.

"Can we have a Halloween party, Dr. Loomis?"

Loomis's eyes all but bulged out of their
sockets. "A Halloween party! You of all people..."

"All the other kids think it would be a wonderful idea. So does Nurse Kramer, and Dr. Martin said he'd have no objection."

"Nurse Kramer and Dr. Martin are my subordinates, and they . . ."

"Are you sure you don't want us to have one?" Michael asked. His feelings were clearly very strong.

"Of course I'm . . ." He caught himself in mid-sentence, and suddenly he realized a Halloween party might be just the thing. A plan formed in his mind, and after a moment's reflection he said, "Well, actually, I see no harm."

The mere announcement of the party proved therapeutic for most of the boys in the ward as they set to work industriously to create costumes and decorations. The costumes they chose were revealing of their deepest fantasies, and this was an unexpected bonus for the psychiatric staff who might otherwise have had to probe for months into their minds for the same material.

In the last week before Halloween, Michael began to get restless and excited, edgy and irascible. Loomis was well aware of the psychiatric phenomenon known as the "anniversary syndrome," wherein mentally disturbed persons relive the events of the previous year's trauma. Michael seemed to be following this classic pattern, and on the evening of October 31, Loomis placed the staff on what he only half-jokingly called red alert. The children (the girl's ward had been allowed to join the boys for the occasion) were to be carefully observed, and Loomis wanted two staff members besides himself to do nothing else but watch Michael. Loomis needed not only an incident, but witnesses.

The children were led into the little gymnasium, where black and orange streamers had been festooned, and cutouts of witches and goblins, black cats and pumpkins made by the children had been taped to the walls. The children wore their costumes, and even the nurses and orderlies donned clever masks, hats, or costumes to join in the fun.

Michael was dressed as a clown.

After cake and soda, the games began. For obvious reasons, they were kept simple and nonthreatening. But after a round of musical chairs, in which a sixteen-year-old girl named Sophie had beaten Michael out for the last chair (had she known about the boy's reputation, she'd have given it to him), Loomis leaned forward alertly, scrutinizing Michael. The stage had been set for *something*.

The next game was ducking for apples. A huge vat had been borrowed from the kitchen, filled with water, and a dozen apples floated in it. The idea was for the children to pick an apple out of the water using just their teeth.

After eight or nine children had gone, it was Sophie's turn. Michael stood third or fourth in line behind her. She leaned over the lip of the vat, struggling to keep her hands behind her back to resist the temptation to grab the apple.

The lights went out.

It was not uncommon for the lights to fail at Smith's Grove, especially on windy nights, when trees fell on power lines in rural areas. But it was not a windy night.

Loomis had been prepared for anything but this. He leapt from his chair and ran in the pitch darkness for the spot where he thought the vat was. He bowled over several shrieking children and groped the last few steps until he collided with the platform on which the vat stood. At that moment the hospital's own emergency generators, which tripped on automatically when the main utility system failed, brought light back into the auditorium.

Sophie lay face down beside the vat, drenched

from the waist up. Loomis searched the room for
Michael. He stood under a basketball backboard,
at least ten steps away, smiling. Loomis looked at
the boy's costume and hands: They were completely dry.

With a nurse Loomis applied artificial res-
piration, and after a moment the girl brought up
a large quantity of water, sputtering and gasping.

The party was over. Loomis's trap had failed.

But ultimately, Loomis won. For, on the day
he was scheduled to drive up to the county seat
to plead his case with Judge Christopher, he re-
ceived a phone call from the bailiff of the juvenile
court.

The night before, Judge Christopher had had
a massive coronary and died on the way to the
hospital.

Judge Christopher's successor was far less
sympathetic to Michael Myers. He had only read
about the case, and was convinced Michael was
the brutal killer that the psychiatrist claimed.
Loomis presented the new judge with a forty-five-
page paper describing Michael's personality and
the incidents of the last year, and though there
was still not a shred of evidence to support Loomis's contention that Michael was a homicidal psy-
chopath, the new judge accepted Loomis's opinion
that it was best to keep the boy behind institu-
tional walls.

And so it was that fifteen years passed . . .

5

On the evening of October 30, 1978, a new Buick station wagon sliced through the blackness of a rainy night on State Highway 116, heading east toward the Smith's Grove state facility. On the front door of the sleek car was the institution's emblem. The only other thing that distinguished it from an ordinary car was the chickenwire grating that separated the front and back seats.

Inside, her face illuminated by the eerie glow of the dashboard and the occasional orange light of her passenger's nervously puffed cigarettes, Marion Treadwell, R.N., peered into the jet night. She wore a crisply starched white nurse's uniform and hat, and a navy cape with red piping around her shoulders. Her knuckles on the steering wheel were white. As if she weren't nervous enough about tonight's assignment, the foul weather made her as uptight as a drug addict looking for a score.

As her passenger smoked and talked, Marion resisted the temptation to look at him. She'd heard so much about Dr. Loomis, both good and bad, and after glimpsing him when she'd picked him up in front of his home she could see why he was spoken of with that mixture of reverence and dread that people reserved for a Rasputin. His head was shaved bald, but he wore a gray goatee, giving him a slightly diabolical appearance. He dressed

in a limp, wrinkled brown suit and not-very-rain-
proof trench coat, and apparently gave no heed
whatever to the conventions of good dress. His
crystal blue eyes were awesome in their intensity,
and you knew at once that mundane matters like
proper attire were beneath the interest of a man
with such eyes.

In his lap he held a manila folder whose notes
he tried to follow with his index finger in the light
emanating from the dashboard. ". . . Then he
gets another physical examination by the state,
followed by an appearance before the judge. Bear
in mind that this is not the judge of the juvenile
court, because the subject is no longer a minor.
In any case, the procedure should take four hours
if we're lucky. Then we're on our way. As before,
he will be heavily sedated."

"What did you use before?"

"Thorazine."

The driver frowned. "Why, he'll barely be
able to sit up."

Loomis smiled grimly. "That's the idea.
Here we are." He gestured toward a large white
sign fixed to a low brick wall on the left. It said:

Smith's Grove
Warren County Sanitarium

Through the blackness and the downpour she
could make out the shadowy mass of the institution looming up on the hillside surrounded by a
sturdy steel fence above which ran three strips of
no-nonsense barbed wire.

"The driveway's up a few hundred yards on
your right," Loomis indicating, gesturing with
his cigarette.

The nurse, an attractive redhead, was slightly disappointed that Loomis hadn't asked her
anything about herself. She guided the station
wagon around the approach road. Loomis's indica-

tion that he intended to keep their charge
drugged was typical of the rumors she'd heard
about this rugged-jawed, single-minded man. It
was said that the patients he treated successfully
returned to the world completely adjusted and capable of leading normal lives. It was also said that
those he thought incapable of recovery, he sedated until they were no more dangerous than a
row of stringbeans. "Are there any special instructions?" she asked.

For the first time he looked at her directly.
"Just try to understand what we're dealing with
here. Don't underestimate it."

Her eyes narrowed. "Don't you think we
should refer to 'it' as 'him'?"

Loomis shrugged. "If you say so," he said
without conviction.

"Your compassion is overwhelming, Doctor,"
she said, reaching for a pack of cigarettes. She
took one out and slipped it between her full lips.
Then she groped for her matches. Loomis reached
into his coat for his lighter, but she found her
matches first and lit her own cigarette. Now
Loomis did look at her for the first time, noting
the sheen of her auburn hair, the high cheek-
bones, the pert nose, as the flare of the match
momentarily illuminated her attractive features.
She put the matches up on the dashboard, but
they slipped off as the car lurched to the right.
Loomis picked them up off the carpeted floor. They
said, "The Rabbit-in-Red Lounge—Entertainment Nightly." An odd name, he thought, and
wondered whether the young lady frequented the
place and what sort of entertainment one might
be fortunate enough to see there.

"Ever done anything like this before?" he
asked.

"Only minimum security."

"I see," he said, failing to keep the pity out
of his voice.

"What does that mean?" she said defensively, picking up his tone.

"It means . . ." He gazed at her, assessing her maturity and concluding she didn't have too much of it. "It means *I see,* that's all."

"You don't have to make this any harder than it already is," she said forthrightly.

Loomis's smile was devoid of humor. "I couldn't if I tried."

"The only thing that ever bothers me is their gibberish. When they start raving on and on . . ." She finished the thought with a shiver and a look of disgust.

"You don't have to worry about that," said Loomis. "He's scarcely spoken a word in years."

Suddenly, in the middle distance, the car's headlights detected a ghostly shape about twenty-five yards away. Loomis leaned forward and peered, eyebrows knit in dismay. "Something is wrong."

Marion lifted her foot from the gas pedal and hovered it over the brake, awaiting instructions as she squinted through the windshield into the troubled night. The wraithlike figure had momentarily disappeared. Then five of them appeared. Patients clad in windblown, rain-soaked white gowns, wandering or cavorting around the field outside the fence. Their eyes were hollow and almost zombielike, their faces ravaged by decades of incarceration.

"Since when do they let them wander around?" Marion asked cynically.

"They don't," Loomis replied unnecessarily, gesturing impatiently for her to drive the rest of the way to the gate, where there was a telephone. "Drive, drive!"

A figure stepped in front of them, a male patient with an insane grin and red-rimmed eyes. Marion had to stop the car to avoid running him over. Loomis thrust open his door and jumped

out. He trotted over to the bewildered escapee and
asked him a question. The man gesticulated with
wild, gnarled hands. Loomis's eyes clouded with
fear. He rushed back to the car and hopped in,
rivulets of rain trickling down his bald head into
his face and beard. "Pull up to the entrance!"

"Shouldn't we pick him up?"

"Move it!"

Marion pressed the gas pedal. The rear tires
whined on the wet pavement, then grabbed. The
powerful car almost knocked the hapless inmate
down. "What did he say?"

"He asked me if I could help him find his
purple lawnmower."

"I don't think this is any time to be funny,"
Marion declared indignantly. "After all, I'm . . ."

"He said something else," Loomis said omi-
nously. "He said, 'It's all right now. He's gone.
The evil's gone.' "

They exchanged a serious look. "What does
that mean?"

"Wait here," he said, leaping out of the still-
rolling car and rushing to the guard booth. He
slid the door open and stepped on something soft.
He knelt over it. It was the guard. His head was
twisted on his neck as if some giant hand had
tried to unscrew it. The man's eyes bulged hide-
ously, and his tongue lolled over bloody lips. "My
God!" Loomis gasped as he reached for the phone.

Inside the car, Marion drew nervously on her
cigarette as the escaped inmates did their *danse
macabre* around the parking lot. The driving rain
drummed on the roof and hood, and Loomis's
contorted face in the guard booth as he shouted
his message to the main house did not make her
feel any easier.

All at once there was a tremendous thump on
the roof, which buckled momentarily before popping back into shape. Marion glimpsed a flutter of
white cloth out of the corner of her eye and

realized what it was. "Oh, no, one of them is on the roof of the car," she muttered, rolling the window on the driver's side down to plead with the inmate to get down. The noise on the roof was unimaginable, like someone dancing on it. Marion stuck her head out of the window. "Okay, that'll be enough . . ."

She did not see the powerful hand extending from the roof, but a moment later it had her by the hair and was attempting to pull her through the window. When the intruder realized he couldn't do that, he attempted to get a grip on her jaw to twist her head off.

For a moment she shrieked with helpless panic, but Loomis either didn't see what was happening or couldn't help. There was only one solution before this monstrous hand snapped her neck. She groped desperately for the knob of the window and found it after what seemed an eternity.

She gave it a quarter turn with her free hand, but the problem was that her head was out the window and the man's grip was too strong for her to pull back inside the car. Frantically she clawed at the hand. A finger passed over her open, screaming mouth. She clamped her teeth on it with all her might. The thing let out an inhuman howl and momentarily relaxed its grip. She yanked her head back inside and closed the window on his hand. He roared again and pulled his hand out of the window before her last turn on the knob clamped him irrevocably.

Marion clutched at her throat and gasped for air. She was momentarily safe, but an instant later she had her hands full at the window on the passenger side. The inmate, still on the roof, had struck the window with shattering force, and the window's protective glass had cracked into a thousand geometric splinters that adhered to each other for the moment but would fly into the car the next time he struck it. The thing peered upside down into the car, and Marion saw a ghastly rain-soaked creature made even more horrible by the spiderweb pattern of the cracked window.

Now, in blind panic, she stepped full on the gas pedal. The tires keened on the wet pavement, then took hold and the car lurched forward. Marion tore around the parking lot, hauling the wheel sharply from left to right to left again. The car swayed and skidded, but the thing, clinging to the windshield wiper and a door handle, somehow managed to hold on. The rain cascaded down the windshield and she couldn't see a thing; she certainly didn't see the parking lot curb when she struck it at forty miles an hour. The wheel tore out of her hand and her chin struck the rim. The station wagon spun wildly out of control, hurling her across the seat to the passenger side. Then it struck another curb broadside, and from that moment on Marion remembered nothing until she was being helped to her feet by Loomis. She lay on the soaked grass of an embankment, a violent ringing in her ears, the nerves in her scalp throbbed from the pain of her hair having been violently pulled.

About a dozen paces away the station wagon sat, idling. Loomis examined her and satisfied himself that she'd suffered no serious harm. Then he turned to the car. "Good God, there's someone in there!"

He could see the ghostly shape on the driver's side, and it seemed to be frantically pounding on the steering wheel as if trying to make the thing go. Loomis dashed for the car, but just as he reached it it vaulted forward, careering crazily from side to side until the driver seemed to gain mastery of the controls and roared down the road and onto the highway.

Loomis returned to Marion, who was sobbing hysterically and shuddering from the rain and cold. Pulling her cloak closer around her shoulders, he held her tightly. Together they watched the tail lights of the station wagon fade into the blackness of the Illinois night.

Then he turned to her. "You can calm down now. The evil is gone."

Somehow she took no comfort in that at all.

6

Laurie Strode stepped out of the door of the white frame house on Oak Street and sniffed the air. It was cool and tangy with a faint touch of wood-smoke. Someone had lit a fire in a fireplace some-where down the street, and for Laurie it had a special significance: It marked, in her own mind, the official start of winter. Of course, winter didn't truly begin until the third week in Decem-ber, a little less than two months away, and you couldn't ask for a more autumnal event than Hal-loween, which took place tonight. Nevertheless, Laurie thought about winter, and felt that same mixture of eagerness and dread that most mid-westerners feel about the season.

She was a pretty girl, slim and angular, with straight, brownish-blond hair falling without fan-fare to her shoulders. Farrah hairstyles were all the rage but Laurie thought it was an affectation and a pain in the ass to keep up. Though not exactly a bookworm, she had decided there were simply too many more interesting things to do, like reading, than to spend all that time washing, blow-drying, teasing, and combing, to say noth-ing of dyeing or frosting your hair if you really wanted to do that trip the right way.

She dressed in simple school attire, a print skirt, knee socks, sensible shoes, and a boy's shirt under a sweater. Loaded down under two heavy book bags, she appeared to be round-shouldered and flat-chested, but that didn't worry her. She knew that when she set out to dress and make up for a date, she could hold her own with anybody in her high-school class. But today was a school day and there is no way you can look glamorous on a school day short of getting your own private porter or chauffeur to carry you and your books to school. So you do the best you can, and if your friends tease you about your waddle, you grin and bear it.

She was slightly surprised to note several younger children already dressed in Halloween costumes. Then she realized they were not trick-or-treating at eight in the morning, but merely dressed up for Halloween parties at school. Her cool blue eyes warmed as two little six-year-old girls with eminently solemn faces glided by in satin gowns and rhinestone tiaras, turning occasionally to bark warnings to the gruff little pirates and cowboys who teased them ten paces behind. She wasn't sure if one of the boys was Tommy Doyle, for whom she was to babysit tonight.

Babysitting. Number one boring job. *Boring!* Some of her girl friends used babysitting as a means for making out. Perhaps if Laurie were interested in somebody she might do the same thing, but there wasn't anyone in her life right now, so it looked like she would be spending another evening supervising Tommy's addiction to horror movies and satisfying his craving (and, she admitted, her own) for popcorn.

She thought about what her girl friends did with their dates on babysitting jobs. Some of them had confessed—even boasted—that they went all the way with their boyfriends. Laurie wasn't inexperienced, and she wasn't a prude either, but she knew herself well enough to understand she wouldn't be able to handle that trip at

the tender age of seventeen. In fact, she sometimes wondered if there was something wrong
with her, if she was a little retarded or something.
The smoldering fires of adolescence had never
really tortured her body the way it did some of
her friends (like Annie, for instance). And although almost everybody in her class smoked
grass, she not only had never gotten high, she
couldn't draw the smoke into her lungs without
coughing. And she was too smart to be interested
in any other kind of drug.

"Laurie, Laurie," she said under her breath,
shaking her head morosely, "at this rate you'll
end up to be as sensible as your mother. What a
drag!"

"What are you dreaming about, sweetheart?"
came her father's voice from behind. Chester
Strode stood on the front doorstep, fooling with
a keyring.

"Oh, the usual: sex and drugs," she laughed,
knowing he wouldn't take her seriously.

"Thank goodness," he said. "I was worried
you were O.D.-ing on English lit and political sci-
ence."

"No danger of that," she retorted. "My parents brought me up to be a straight and decent
kid."

They walked together to his car, a black sedan with "Strode Real Estate" emblazoned in
bold red and white on the door. It never failed
to embarrass her, this advertisement glaring at
people wherever they drove. Maybe things like
this were done in Cleveland or Chicago or St.
Louis, but in a small town like Haddonfield most
people kept a low profile. Oh well, it brought daddy business, and (as her father was fond of pointing out) business meant food and clothes and a
college education. So she couldn't really complain.

They stood beside the car for a moment until

her father managed to slide the proper key off his ring, which had so many keys on it (he called it his occupational affliction) he looked like a jailer. Handing a simple brass key to her, he said, "Now don't forget to drop this off at the Myers place."

"I won't," she said. She decided to keep it in her hand instead of dropping it into her book bag, where it would be "out of sight, out of mind."

"They're coming by to see the house at ten-thirty. Be sure you leave it under the mat."

"I promise."

She started to walk away.

"Haven't you forgotten something?" he called after her. He stood by the car, head tilted, exposing his freshly shaved cheek.

Laurie walked back and put her lips hastily to his cheek, hoping none of her girl friends was watching, then feeling guilty immediately afterward. Why should a girl be embarrassed about kissing her own father, for crying out loud?

She sat out down Oak Street, rolling slightly from side to side with the weight of her books— the famous Laurie Waddle. In her right hand the key to the Myers house seemed to tingle, and suddenly she found herself thinking about the house. It was the one property her father handled that he was ashamed to speak of, and his relief at unloading it for once far outweighed his profit motive. For this was the house in which a seventeen-year-old girl had been brutally slain by her little brother fifteen years ago.

The Myerses had moved away a few months after the tragedy. The grief, shame, and harassment by the press and gawking neighbors and passersby had made their lives in Haddonfield intolerable. From somewhere in Indiana they continued to pay their mortgage loan and taxes, which, as Laurie's father had often said, was a terrible double burden. Not only could they not find a buyer all those years, but they had to bear the emotional burden every time they wrote out a check to support the unsaleable house.

Chester Strode had used every trick in his prodigious salesman's bag to sell The White Turkey, as he'd come to call it. But as soon as prospective buyers heard about the events of October 31, 1963, from neighbors all too eager to tell them, their superstition invariably got the best of them and it was good-bye sale. Mr. Strode couldn't even persuade customers to buy the property for the value of the land. "Buy it and raze the house, if that's the way you feel," he would tell them. But the property was tainted, and no one went for the bait.

Thank God for the New York couple who thought the house was just what they were looking for, and who were too sophisticated to believe the nonsense the neighbors prattled about. In fact, the New York couple actually thought the idea of a haunted house was charming, something they could boast about. So Mr. Strode gave the New Yorkers something else they could boast about—a price so ridiculous, it was (to use his patented phrase) "lower than a song."

Laurie wondered what it must have been like that night for the Myers girl, seeing her tiny brother coming at her with that enormous butcher knife. Imagine a blade that long going into her stomach, her breasts, her . . . even her . . . ! It was unspeakable, unthinkable.

"Hey, Laurie!"

Rarely had she been so relieved to be pulled out of a fantasy. The caller was Tommy Doyle, the boy she was sitting for tonight. The eight-year-old with tousled brown hair and bright eyes trotted up to her, swinging two or three books strapped together with a belt. Laurie, whose own load of books qualified her to join the Stevedore's Union, sighed at this symbol of vanishing youth. "Hi, Tommy."

He caught up with her and they walked side by side for several paces. "Are you coming over tonight?"

"Same time, same place."

"Can we make jack-o'-lanterns?"

"Sure."

"Can we watch monster movies?"

"Sure."

"Will you read to me? Can we make popcorn?"

"Sure. Sure."

Her answers came absently and automatically. They were the same questions every time, but this time she was thinking about poor Judith Myers as they turned the corner and walked the hundred paces into Peecher Street where the Myers house was. She couldn't purge her mind of that awful picture of a knife, a long, silvery knife, flashing through the air and plunging into her body. A knife wielded by a . . .

"How old are you?"

They had stopped abruptly, and Laurie was staring at the boy. "You know how old I am. I'm eight. Why?"

She hesitated, not wanting to put murderous thoughts into the head of the kid she was sitting for tonight. Yet there was something she had to know. "Have you ever felt like—like killing somebody?"

The boy shrugged. "Sure."

"You *have?*"

"Sure. Hasn't everybody?"

"They *have?*" Her eyes bulged.

"Sure. When somebody takes something away from you, or your parents tell you you can't have something, or the teacher gives you too much homework, you feel like killing them. Is that what you mean?"

"Uh, well . . ."

"Oh, *that's* what you mean!" Tommy said, eyes rounding and the color draining from his face. They had arrived at the Myers house.

It was a ghost of its former self, weather-beaten and dilapidated. Set back from the street twenty or twenty-five paces, it stood glowering in the cool autumn morning like some mangy, brooding beast. Its former spanking coat of white paint, the symbol of pride of every fine midwestern home, had turned to dingy gray, and much of it had peeled or flaked off, revealing a pitted and rotting facade of shingles. Several windows had been broken by kids or vandals, a few of whom had been bold enough to scrawl graffiti on the front door. A huge elm beat against an upstairs window as the breeze stiffened.

"You're not supposed to go up there," the kid said, freezing to the spot.

Laurie flourished the key. "Yes, I am."

"Uh-uh. That's a spook house."

"Just watch," she said, walking coolly up to the porch. She lifted the welcome mat as her father had instructed and placed the key under it. She had wanted Tommy to know how unafraid she was, but if she was so unafraid, why was her hand damp with perspiration as she pulled it back from the mat?

For a moment she stood transfixed, contemplating that night fifteen years ago—"My God, fifteen years ago to the very night!" she realized —when the tragic event had taken place. She vaguely heard Tommy on the sidewalk pleading with her to get away from there, but the horror of it attracted her in some perverse way. Was it the fascination of the innocent with wickedness, or just some sort of sick curiosity? Or was she herself capable of the same gruesome deed?

She shut her eyes and imagined herself picking up a butcher knife and plunging it into the breast of . . . of whom? Whom did she loathe so much she would want to do that to? To someone in your own family, for God's sake! She couldn't think of a soul.

"Laurie, please, I'm getting scared," the boy was whining.

"So am I," she laughed with a shudder, trotting down the porch steps and joining her young companion.

And, as she turned her back on the house, a figure inside it, dark, shadowy, sidled up to the front door and pushed the tattered curtain aside with a knuckle. He watched the slim blonde toss her head and laugh as she raised her hands like a bogeyman to frighten her young companion.

He breathed heavily, raspingly, as he watched the girl, and a memory entered his mind, the memory of another girl, another blonde, willowy and pretty. He remembered the trapped and frightened look in her eyes, and the futile, pathetic way she had raised her hands to protect herself.

He followed the girl and boy with his gaze until they disappeared from view. Then he walked up the creaky stairs to the second floor and peered into the room where it had all happened . . .

"I thought you liked to be scared," Laurie teased Tommy. "God knows, you groove on horror movies enough."

"Yeah, but those are movies. You can always turn the television off if you get *too* scared. You can't turn off real life."

"That's very wise, Tommy."

"Lonnie Elam said never to go up there. Lonnie Elam said it's a haunted house. He told me about some real awful stuff that happened there once."

"Lonnie Elam probably won't get out of third grade."

"I gotta go. I'll see you tonight," Tommy said, breaking away.

"See you."

She paused on the corner, feeling odd, as if someone was boring into the back of her skull. She turned and gazed back at the Myers house. She could just make out the gable of the bedroom where Judith Myers had been killed.

Her eyebrows knit. Was she crazy or was there a shape standing in the window staring at her? She rubbed her eyes and looked again. No, there was nothing there after all. Her imagination was working overtime again. She pivoted and continued down the street to school, trying to stride smartly but rolling with a slight waddle that everybody knew belonged uniquely to Laurie Strode.

7

Sam Loomis strode down the steps of the institution, gesturing to the sky as if invoking the Almighty to help the fool beside him understand. The other man, gray-haired and ashen-faced, shrank before Loomis's wrath.

"I'm *not* responsible, Sam," Dr. Wynn pleaded unconvincingly.

"Of course not."

"I've given them his profile."

Loomis stopped in his tracks and stared at the sanitarium's chief administrator. "You gave them the profile of a village idiot, not a homicidal maniac. Two roadblocks and an all-points bulletin wouldn't stop a five-year-old!" He all but ran back to his car, again hurling imprecations to the sky. "I sometimes wonder who needs shock treatments more, the patients or the staff!"

"He was your patient, Doctor," Wynn argued halfheartedly as Loomis unlocked his car door. "If the precautions weren't sufficient, you should have notified . . ."

"I notified everybody. You have a file on that man six inches thick. Either you don't read these things or you can't. Oh, God, save me from these bureaucrats!" He slipped quickly into the car and fumbled for his keys.

"There's nothing I can do," the hapless Wynn said.

"That's certain. You did nothing before, why should you be able to do anything now? How about getting on the telephone and telling them exactly what got out of here last night? And tell them where he's going."

"We don't know what got out of here last night. Your six-inch-thick file is full of conjecture. As for where he's going, that's conjecture too."

"You call that guard's broken neck conjecture? Tell that to his widow! You call the assault on the nurse conjecture? He pulled half the hair out of her scalp, for Christ's sake."

"The police will catch him."

"If they look for him in Haddonfield, they might."

Wynn flashed a patronizing smile that enraged Loomis even more. "Sam, Haddonfield is a hundred and fifty miles from here. How could he get there? He can't drive."

"He was doing all right last night. Maybe somebody around here gave him lessons. If you read the file you know that he had the run of the place. Inmates and staff alike were scared to death of him and indulged his every wish. Someone could very well have taught him how to drive."

"That's preposterous. If he had so much freedom, why didn't he walk out of here years ago?"

"Because he had it made here. He had his little empire."

Wynn shook his head and rolled his eyes heavenward, as exasperated with Loomis as Loomis was with him. "Then why did he take off from here all of a sudden?"

"Because . . ." Loomis had a strong idea why: for the same reason why he was probably heading for Haddonfield. But if Wynn hadn't bought any of Loomis's explanations up to now, he sure as hell wouldn't accept any now. "I don't know why," Loomis snapped. "Why won't you announce this to the press?"

"You know why."

Loomis clapped his hand to his skull. "Yes, it looks bad for the hospital. You're willing to let a butcher roam the countryside so you can save your job. Oh, *God*, save me from bureaucrats!" he repeated more fervently. He started the car and rolled down the window. "I tell you this, *Doctor* Wynn, when the bodies start turning up, your job won't be worth an orderly's salary. You'll be lucky they don't send you to prison for gross negligence." He rolled up the window, jammed the shift into drive, and skittered out of the parking lot like a drag racer.

About three miles down the highway he was flagged down by a state policeman, who peered casually into the back seat and didn't even bother to make Loomis open the trunk. Loomis shook his head sadly and roared away from the roadblock, steering the nose of his car toward Haddonfield.

After an hour he came to a sign announcing "Haddonfield 73 miles," beside which was a telephone booth. Just beyond it, a red pickup truck was parked. The door of the dilapidated vehicle was open, but Loomis could not see anyone.

Loomis frowned and pulled over to kill several birds with one stone. He had to phone his wife, he had to take a leak, and he wanted to look at the truck with the open door.

In order of least importance, he called his wife.

"No," he said after a few familiar homilies, "not since Thursday . . . Yes, I'm all right. Stop worrying. After this I'll sleep for a week, two weeks. But for now, I must stop him. Of course it's possible," he replied to a conjecture as fatuous as some of Wynn's, "but I know him. And when he gets there, God help us." He gave her some more time-wasting assurances, drumming his fingers impatiently on the coin box. Then, as he was about to ring off, he said, "Oh, listen, dear. When they come around trick-or-treating tonight, why don't you just not answer the door. I *know* it's ridiculous, but just this once?"

He hung up and walked to a mound of high grass hidden from the road and relieved his burdened bladder, then went over to the truck to examine it. Perhaps it was merely one abandoned months ago. On the other hand . . .

On the seat lay a newspaper. Loomis pulled it out and looked at the date: October 30, 1978. Yesterday's.

He was about to return it to the seat when he noticed a crushed cigarette pack and a pack of matches half obscured by the dirt at his feet. He stooped to pick them up and read the message on the matchbook with fear clawing his heart: "The Rabbit-in-Red Lounge—Entertainment Nightly."

He raced back to the car, jumped in, started it, and roostertailed back onto the highway.

About six paces beyond where he'd urinated, a man lay in the grass. Except for his shorts, he was naked. His eyes stared in sightless horror at the clouds that had begun to roll in the sky. His body, however, lay stomach downward.

8

". . . And the book ends, but what Samuels is really talking about here is fate."

Mrs. Fredericks shut the book with a thump, then went to the blackboard and with the side of a piece of chalk wrote the word *fate* in large bold letters. She then wrote the name *Rollins* in smaller letters about three feet away from *fate*, and connected the two with four arrows going from *Rollins* to *fate*, one of them direct, the other three describing large arcs.

Laurie had not been paying much attention to the morning lesson, for her mind kept drifting to the image of a six-year-old boy with a gleaming butcher knife plunging it again and again into the softness of her body. Her legs were crossed and she squeezed her thighs tightly together to keep the imagined blade from making its most horrifying thrust of all.

She looked down at her notebook and realized the symbolism of the doodles she'd been making absently during the teacher's exposition of the novel: dagger-shaped arrows penetrating a Valentinelike heart. Perhaps that was why she sat up attentively when she noticed the arrows Mrs. Fredericks had drawn on the blackboard. They all extended from *Rollins,* and all went in different directions. Yet all ultimately arrived at *fate*.

"You see," Mrs. Fredericks amplified, "fate

caught up with several lives here. No matter what
course of action Rollins took, he was destined to
meet his own fate, his own day of reckoning. The
idea is that destiny is a very real, concrete thing
that every person has to deal with." She em-
phasized this by stabbing at the word *fate* five
times in rapid succession with the chalk until it
snapped. Two or three students giggled, but Laurie drew her breath in sharply.

She mused about fate. Suppose it was my
fate to die like Judith Myers. No matter which
way I ran, no matter what I tried, that blade
would be waiting for me. Gosh, that couldn't be
my fate. I'm too young. I'm too, well, too nice.
But Judith Myers was young, and probably no
less nice than I. It was just her destiny, that's all.
It had been determined by God a million years
ago that on October 31, 1963, Judith Myers would
be horribly murdered. But why would God do a
thing like that to a nice girl? God wouldn't do
anything evil like that, would He? We were
taught in Sunday school . . .

As her mind wandered dreamily over these
solemn questions, she noticed a station wagon
parked on the street. Behind the wheel, gazing
into her classroom, gazing it seemed directly at
her, was a man. At least she thought it was a man.
He was dressed as far as she could make out in
dark khaki mechanics coveralls. His hair was
black, but his face seemed preternaturally white,
almost powdered. In fact, the more she looked at
the face, with its red lips and sunken purple eyes,
she wondered if he weren't wearing a mask.
He'd better be, because if that's his own face,
that guy is in *trouble*. Wow, if he's looking at
me, then *I'm* in trouble!

Hoping he would go away, she focused on
Mrs. Fredericks, who had picked up her broken
chalk and was putting some finishing touches on
her rendering of *Man against His Fate*, underlin-

ing and circling *fate* several more times. As she'd
had enough morbid thoughts for one day or for a
lifetime, Laurie concentrated on the lesson. "Ed-
win," Mrs. Fredericks was asking, "how does
Samuels's view of fate differ from that of Costain?"

I'm not going to look at that man, Laurie
swore to herself as the boy two rows away muttered an answer. I can see him out of the corner
of my eye, but I'm not going to give him the sat-
isfaction of looking at him. Well, maybe just a bit
to see if he's still . . .

She turned her head ever so slightly.

He was.

"Laurie?"

The pronunciation of her name came like a
thunderclap, and she jumped as if a bolt had
struck her seat. "Ma'am?"

"Perhaps you can answer the question."

She closed her eyes and brought the question into the forefront of her mind. Then she
struggled for a moment to produce an answer.

"Uh . . . Costain wrote that fate was somehow
related only to religion." The teacher's smile of
approbation prompted Laurie to go on and gave
her fortitude. "Whereas, Samuels felt that fate
was like a natural element, like earth, air, fire,
and water."

"That's right," said Mrs. Fredericks. "Samuels definitely personified fate . . ."

He was gone.

She'd decided, even as she spoke to the class,
that she was going to whip her head around when
she finished and glare at him, whoever he was, until he dropped his eyes in embarrassment.

But he was gone.

He was back.

Several hours later, as school ended with a
blaring alarm bell, he sat in the stolen station

wagon, watching the children burst out of the doors with a clamor. Many of them were dressed in Halloween costumes and bore black and orange paper cutouts made in school, witches and pumpkins, black cats and devils, skeletons and ghosts. One little girl pretended to be riding a broomstick with a cardboard black cat on it, another wore a jack-o'-lantern on his head like the famous Headless Horseman.

After a while, four boys emerged, one of them bearing a pumpkin so large he swayed from side to side like an overburdened burro. The other three were pushing him back and forth and taunting him. The boy they were bullying was the same one that had been talking to the pretty blond girl this morning.

"Leave me alone," the boy was pleading.

They wiggled their fingers in his face. "He's gonna getcha, he's gonna getcha, he's gonna getcha!"

The boy slapped at the fingers. "Leave me alone."

"The bogeyman is coming."

"No, he's not. Leave me alone."

"He doesn't believe us. Don't you know what happens on Halloween?" said the biggest one, putting his face close to Tommy's.

Tommy shrugged. "Yeah, we get candy."

They laughed and danced around him, waving their hands in his face. "Oooooh, the bogeyman, oooooh, the bogeyman, the bogeyman, the bogeyman . . ."

Tommy clutched his pumpkin tightly to his chest and tried to push his way through them, but one of them stuck his foot out and tripped him. He fell on top of the pumpkin, which split open with a glupping sound, emitting a sour odor. Tommy had skinned his knee but there was no other damage done except to his pride. He fought back welling tears.

The sound of the boys' cruel laughter faded as they ran away, leaving Tommy to climb painfully to his feet. His jacket was covered with pumpkin pulp and seeds. Suddenly, as he began pulling these off with his fingers, he felt the sunlight eclipsed by a large shadowy figure. He looked up and there was a man in dark khaki coveralls standing there looking at him.

"Hi," said Tommy.

The man said nothing. Tommy could hear him breathing stertorously but the boy couldn't see his face clearly because it was positioned between himself and the sun. What Tommy could make out, however, left him in no mood to hang around. The man had dark red-stained lips and his eyes were rimmed in purple, like grossly overused eyeshadow. A livid scar zig-zagged down his cheek.

The weird thing was, Tommy couldn't imagine that that was the guy's own face. It looked rubbery and kind of masklike. But if he was wearing a mask, shouldn't he take it off around about now and say "Boo!" and reveal who he was?

Tommy didn't like this at all. Grown-ups didn't go prowling around schoolyards wearing masks, Halloween or not. And this guy's breathing sounded like something he'd heard when he'd visited his dying grandpa in the hospital. Creepy! He looked down at the pumpkin, wondering if it could be salvaged.

No way. Meat, pulp, and seeds spilled out of its shattered hull like the contents of a cracked orange skull.

When the man stepped toward him, Tommy needed no inspiration to run like crazy. In a moment his blurred legs had carried him out of the schoolyard and down the street, thinking about the bogeyman.

The man stood indecisively for a moment, then returned to the station wagon. His gait was quick and graceful for a big man. He started the engine and pulled away from the school, turning the corner and accelerating down the street on which the little boy had run. There he was, still running.

He pulled the station wagon parallel to the boy, studying him for a long moment. Then he accelerated again, leaving the kid in his dust. He turned the next corner, then began cruising at random, familiarizing himself with the street patterns—or returning to places dimly remembered ...

"It's *totally* insane!" the leggy blonde was saying. Her hands flew out in a wild gesture, making Laurie laugh. Linda always made Laurie laugh. Just about everything the girl was, everything she did, was so alien to Laurie's thinking and behavior that Linda was like a visitor from another planet. Whereas Laurie's beauty was modestly contained in quiet clothing and hairstyle, Linda wore skin-tight jeans and sweaters and bright ribbons in her hair that virtually shouted *sex here!* to anyone with eyes to see.

Linda had never learned to moderate her voice, so everything she said was an announcement or a declaration, supported by gesticulating hands that never seemed to be burdened by such impediments as books or schoolwork.

The girl's friends had unanimously elected her president of the In-Word of the Month Club. Linda was a lightning rod for trendy phrases, which she used to exhaustion for a month, then dropped from her vocabulary forever, to everyone's immense relief. Three months ago it had been *weird;* two months ago, *gross;* last month, she was calling everyone "Jack." This month's word was *totally*.

"It's totally insane! We have three new cheers to learn in the morning, the game in the

afternoon, I get my hair done at five, and the
dance at eight. I'll be *totally* wiped out!"

"I think you have too much to do tomorrow,"
Laurie observed needlessly.

"Totally!" Linda replied, even more needlessly.

Laurie sighed. "As usual, I don't have anything to do."

"It's your own fault, and I don't feel sorry
for you," Linda declared as they turned a corner
onto a shady avenue. "Look at you, Laurie Strode.
You dress like a fugitive from Miss Prudence's
School for Proper Young Virgins. Your hair is
totally plain. You wear no makeup at all, no eyeshadow, not even lipstick. If you're hoping to
catch a boy, forget it. You couldn't catch a frog
the way you look."

"Thanks a lot!"

"Don't get insulted. You know perfectly well
how pretty I think you are. But you go around
like being pretty is embarrassing. I don't think
anyone in Haddonfield knows if you have any
boobs, you're always hiding them behind a stack
of books that would bring a Sumo wrestler to
his knees, for God's sake! And that walk!"

Laurie was shaking with laughter.
"Enough!"

"That walk!" Linda shouted her down, really
warming to the subject. "With all those books
and bags, you look like a drunken mountain-goat
with an injured . . ."

"Hey Linda, Laurie!"

They didn't have to turn around to recognize Annie's strident voice, which Linda had char-
acterized once as so sharp it could shatter a hero
sandwich. Their inseparable friend slid between
them and their pace doubled. Annie was always
in a rush, though no one was ever able to figure
out why. She rushed to get somewhere and rushed
to get out of there. She rushed to eat, but then

found herself with so much time on her hands she'd complain about being bored. She was dark-haired, with abundant ringlets that glinted auburn in the late afternoon sunlight. She wore a red sweater and a sweater-vest over that, but it did very little to moderate the thrust of a very large pair of breasts that jiggled unharnessed beneath the fabric. Despite the trends, most of the teenage girls in Haddonfield chose not to disdain bras, either because of traditional midwestern modesty or parental restrictions. But Annie, whose father was the town sheriff, cared not a whit about traditional midwestern modesty *or* parental restrictions. She not only had been the first of her crowd to abandon her bra, she had been the first to abandon her virginity. Linda had been the second to sleep with a boy, and now the two girls talked about "it" like connoisseurs talking about three-star French restaurants.

"Why didn't you wait for me?" Annie panted.

"We did," said Linda. "Fifteen minutes. You never showed up."

"That's not true. Here I am."

"What's wrong?" Laurie asked. "You're not smiling."

"I'll never smile again. Paul dragged me into the boy's locker room . . ."

"I'd smile plenty if a boy did that to me!" Linda said exuberantly.

"Exploring uncharted territory?" Laurie asked.

"It's been totally charted," Linda remarked, giggling.

"No, he dragged me in there to talk to me."

"You just talked, huh?"

"We just talked."

"Sure," both girls said in unison.

"Honest. Old Jerko got caught throwing eggs and soaping windows. His parents grounded him for the weekend. He can't come over tonight," Annie sighed, almost ready to cry.

"I thought you were babysitting tonight," Laurie said.

Linda sneered. "The only reason she babysits is to have a place to . . ."

"Shit!" Laurie cried, snapping her fingers.

"I *have* a place for that," Annie said, mock-indignantly.

"No, I forgot my chemistry book."

"Who cares?" Linda laughed. "I *always* forget my chemistry book!"

"You forget everything but your pill," Annie teased.

Laurie turned on her heels, wondering if it was worth it to run back to school to get her book. Maybe she could just borrow one.

The station wagon turned into the street and cruised slowly toward them. Laurie frowned. This was the same car that that spooky man had been in when Laurie spotted him from the window of her English Lit class. She peered at the figure in the driver's seat, but the glint of late afternoon sunlight and the reflection of trees on the windshield made identification impossible.

The girls turned to look too as the driver gunned his engine and glided by, staring at them.

"Isn't that Davon Graham?" Linda said, squinting. "He's cute."

"I don't think so," said Laurie, noting again the strange pale face with eyes limned in dark purple. A moment later the car whizzed by, leaving the three gaping at what they thought they'd seen behind the wheel.

"Speed kills!" Annie yelled at the driver.

All of a sudden the car screeched to a halt. The figure sat there, waiting.

The girls stood on the sidewalk hesitantly. Usually they'd pile into a passing car that stopped for them, even if they only remotely knew the guy. But there was something unsettling about this situation. "Can't you take a joke?" Annie said, addressing the car but making sure the driver didn't hear her.

He stared at them, making them intensely uncomfortable, as if he had the power to see through clothing. Then, to their relief, he stepped on the gas and took off down the street, disappearing around a corner.

Laurie shook her head. "Annie, some day you're going to get all of us in deep trouble."

"Totally!" Linda agreed, putting a hand over her chest and hyperventilating.

"I hate a guy with a car and no sense of humor."

"That's the only kind you date," said Linda.

They strolled on, their spirits somewhat subdued by their encounter. Laurie was pensive and troubled. Something was wrong. That man . . . the figure in the window of the Myers house . . . Halloween . . . a butcher knife blurring toward her . . .

Meanwhile, her friends chattered on.

"Well," Linda was saying, "are we still on for tonight?"

"I wouldn't want to get you in *deep* trouble, Linda," Annie replied.

"Come on, Annie. Bob and I have been planning on it all week."

Annie sighed. "All right. The Wallaces leave at seven."

Laurie made a conscious effort to pull her mind away from its morbid fixation. "I'm babysitting for the Doyles. It's right across the street. We can keep each other company."

"Terrific," Annie groaned. "I've got three choices. Watch the kid sleep, listen to Linda screw, or talk to you." They stopped in front of

Linda's house, a pastel green frame house with dark green shutters. It was nestled beneath a towering elm whose leaves twirled to the prim lawn with every gust of the autumn breeze. "What time?" Annie asked, without enthusiasm.

"I don't know yet," Linda replied. "I have to get out of taking my stupid brother trick-or-treating."

"Saving the treats for Bob?" Annie asked gaily.

"Fun-ny. See you." Linda walked up the path to her house, her tightly clad rear end jiggling seductively.

"You don't have to wiggle it," Annie called out to her, "there aren't any guys around."

"You can never tell when one may be hiding in the bushes," Linda replied, shouldering the front door and disappearing inside.

Annie and Laurie started up the street again, Annie launching into a tirade about Paul's stupidity in getting himself grounded on one of the key weekends in the year. As she rattled on, Laurie saw the figure again.

At least she thought she did. About fifty yards down the street, something was standing at the edge of a tall hedgerow separating two homes. The khaki green of his coveralls blended so well with the olive color of the bushes that for a moment she thought it was merely an extension of the shrubbery. Then she glimpsed the ghostly white face through the leaves. "Look!"

"Look where?"

"Behind that bush there?"

Laurie pointed to . . .

. . . an empty spot beside the hedgerow.

"You're going to tell me there was a guy in the bushes, right?"

"There was."

"Very funny. A second after Linda says there

may be a guy hiding in the . . . really, Laurie.
Your sense of humor . . ."

"I'm telling you. The man who drove by, the
one you yelled at?"

"Subtle, isn't he? Hey, creep!" Annie raced
down the street ahead of her friend, balling her
fist to slug the masher lurking in the bushes. She
peeked around and . . . A cunning smile came over
Annie's face. "Hey, Laurie, he wants to talk to
you," she shouted. Laurie stood riveted to the
sidewalk. "He wants to take you out tonight!"

Laurie approached the hedge cautiously,
knees tensed to catapult her out of there quickly.
Like a timid kitten, she peered around the hedge.
Nobody there. "Very funny, to use your expression."

"One practical joke deserves another."

"He was standing right here."

"Poor Laurie," Annie commiserated, "you
scared another one away." She petted her friend
on the head.

"Cute."

They ambled down the street, Laurie looking
skittishly behind her and approaching another
hedgerow with trepidation.

Annie became serious. "It's tragic. You never
go out. You must have a small fortune stashed
from babysitting. What's your story? You scared?
I'll show you how to relax. You prefer girls? I'll
try anything once."

Laurie laughed, then shrugged. "Guys think
I'm too smart."

"I don't. I think you're whacko. You're seeing
men behind bushes!" They stopped before a pretty
ranch home partially masked from the street by a
pair of dogwood trees. "Well, home sweet home.
I'll see you."

"Okay. 'Bye."

"I'll call you or you call me."

"Right," said Laurie, approaching the last privet hedge on the street with steeled legs. She leaned around it, inch by inch.

Nobody.

She looked behind her, walking backward as she scanned the street for the mysterious figure or his station wagon.

Suddenly a hand gripped her arm.

She screamed, dropping her books. She tried to run but the hand clutched her arm too tightly. Over her right shoulder she caught the shadow of a big man. Vaguely remembering some judo moves her gym teacher had taught her class for warding off would-be rapists, she shifted her weight, grasped the man's wrist, and stuck her leg between his. She started to roll forward. *"Unggg,"* she groaned, as the man stood his ground effortlessly. Momentarily she expected to feel the cold steel of his blade plunging into her stomach or slicing across her throat. Then she noticed the color of his sleeve.

Navy blue.

She relaxed and the hand released her. She whirled around and almost collapsed with relief in the arms of Sheriff Lee Brackett, Annie's father.

The handsome, ruddy-faced man in the blue trooper's uniform laughed. "You won't win a black belt that way."

Laurie sighed loudly. "Mister Brackett! Thank God!"

"You were maybe expecting the bogeyman?"

"I don't know what I was expecting."

"I'm sorry, honey. I didn't mean to startle you."

"It's okay."

"Well," he said, stooping to help her pick up her scattered books, "it's Halloween. I guess everybody's entitled to a good scare."

"Yes, sir."

"But look here. Next time someone comes up to you from behind like that, here's the way that throw is supposed to go."

He stood in front of her and demonstrated the classic move.

"For one thing, you used the wrong foot. No leverage that way. Here, put your books down for a second."

Laurie set them down, then positioned herself in front of Brackett, who must have been six foot two and close to two hundred pounds. "I think I could toss an oak tree easier than I could budge you!" she laughed nervously.

"Some ancient Greek said, 'Give me a lever long enough and I could move the world.' It's all in leverage."

Laurie blinked. "I'm impressed. Where'd you learn about the ancient Greeks?"

Brackett laughed. "You'd be surprised how smart dumb cops are. Now," he said, placing her in front of him, "put *this* foot here, grab me by the arms *this* way, then roll with your full weight . . . *whoa!*" Laurie threw her hip out and tossed the big man over her shoulder onto the lawn.

"Oh, Lord, I'm sorry, Mr. Brackett. I didn't realize . . ."

"Your own strength? That's the whole idea. I think!" he added, raising himself to his feet and brushing himself off. "Well, now you're ready for the bogeyman." He stooped to pick up her books again.

"Thanks, Mr. Brackett. Tell Annie I'll speak to her tonight."

"You bet." Still dusting leaves off his uniform, he ambled home.

She turned into her street, reflecting on the day's strange occurrences. "Well, kiddo," she said to herself, "I thought you outgrew superstition." For a moment, before she stepped onto the flagstone path to her front door, she observed a group of kids parading down the street in their goofy, store-bought costumes and wondered where it had all started, these traditions: witches, hobgoblins, pumpkins, and black cats. And she had to admit she knew no more about Halloween than she knew about judo throws—less, since she knew at least how to throw one sheriff if he stood still long enough.

Dimly she realized that the celebration must hearken back to the times when evil was more respected in the world. She'd seen *The Exorcist* and *The Omen,* and she knew it was possible that evil and its incarnations—like ghosts, the devil, and witches—really existed. But she'd never met anyone who truly believed it, and deep down she certainly didn't believe it herself. But what had changed since the time when priests had performed exorcisms, when people were afraid to go into cemeteries and attended rituals to make the devil appear or chase the devil away?

Have I ever known anything truly evil? she asked herself. Except for Mrs. Langholm's history tests, Laurie couldn't think of a thing.

Yes, there *was* one thing.

Something genuinely wicked had happened in this very town fifteen years ago, only a few blocks from where she now stood. There was no other way to describe the horror of a sweet little six-year-old boy stalking up to the room of a pretty, ordinary teenage girl and running a long knife into her guts dozens of times. That was evil. There was no other word for it.

With a shudder, she stepped into her house. "Hi, Mom, I'm home."

"Hi, darling." Laurie went into the kitchen, where her mother, a redheaded woman with the same angular slenderness of her daughter, was busy candying apples.

Laurie unloaded her books on the kitchen counter and stretched her weary arms. She kissed her mother and dipped a finger in the apple glaze, touching it to her tongue. "Mom, have you ever known anyone evil?"

Her mother cocked her head and looked at Laurie with arched eyebrows. "That's quite a question!"

"Well?"

Her mother washed her gooey fingertips in the sink, then wiped them on a paper towel. "Well, they said that Hitler was evil, but I was too young to remember the war, and of course the only thing I know about his atrocities is what I've read or seen in the movies. I mean, I've never experienced someone evil, if that's what you're getting at."

"I think it is. What about the little boy who stabbed the Myers girl?"

Mrs. Strode shook her head. "You're certainly thinking some dark thoughts today, young lady."

"I know."

"But it's interesting that you mention it. If you went to church more often, you'd understand why."

"Huh?"

"Yes. You see, the Myers case was mentioned by Reverend Peters in last Sunday's sermon."

"It was?" Laurie leaned forward, fascinated.

"Uh-huh. He started off reminding us that Halloween was coming up this week, and he said some real interesting things about the origins of Halloween, about how it goes back to festivals aimed at warding off demons at harvest time, way back when."

"What does that have to do with the Myers case?"

"Well, Reverend Peters said the Myers case, which happened on Halloween fifteen years ago, reminds us that true evil still exists in this world. He said that like everything else, we've tried to deodorize evil and put it in a bright new package

and you can buy it at the supermarket for five
cents off with a coupon. Then along comes something like the Myers case and we're left with our
mouths open looking into the . . . what'd he call
it? . . . the heart of darkness. Maybe that's why
God put devils like the Myers kid on earth—to
keep us aware of the darker side of human nature.
And maybe you ought to do some studying. I
doubt if you'll get much homework done tonight."

"Thanks, Mom. That was real interesting,
what you said." Her mother looked at her skeptically, but Laurie had no mischievous look on her
face. "No, I really mean it." She hauled her books
up from the kitchen counter and lumbered upstairs.

"Are you sure you're not coming down with
something?" Mrs. Strode called after her.

"No, just a minor case of the spooks. It's
Halloween, after all."

She dumped her books on her desk and made
a beeline for her phone for her daily gossip fix, as
she called it. The phone stood on a table near the
side window of her room, which looked down on
a pair of driveways belonging to her own house
and the one next door. On sunny days her mother
often hung laundry on a line there.

She looked idly out the window as she dialed
two digits. Then she gasped and put the phone
sharply back on its cradle.

He was there.

Partially masked by flapping sheets, he stood
there looking up at her window. His face was
flour-white, his lips rouge-red, his eyes dark and
limitless. The texture of his skin was rubbery
looking, but it was still impossible to tell if he was
wearing a mask. Until this moment she'd had a
sneaking suspicion it might be Eddie Lester or
Paul Sheehan or one of those clowns who were always pulling practical jokes. And except April
Fool's, when they worked overtime at it, if ever

there was a day for practical jokes, Halloween was it.

But no, this person was different. He was huskier than any of the guys at school. And there was something about the way he hung back instead of tearing off his mask, identifying himself and saying the joke was over, the way any normal prankster would. And this person was so elusive. You looked at him and he was there, but if you blinked he was gone. And that station wagon. She'd never seen it around, and she and her friends knew every car in town, for sure. She'd noticed some kind of emblem on the door as it cruised past this afternoon. Next time it went by she'd look at it more carefully, or try to get the license number.

But now . . .

Now he was gone.

Biting her lip, she slammed the window down hard, rattling the sash, and locked it. Rubbing her knuckles over her teeth, she paced around her room, wondering what to do. She twisted her head suddenly toward the window to catch him unawares, but he was gone. She began to doubt her senses.

Her phone rang, making her jump as if a shotgun had gone off at her feet. She picked it up. "Hello?"

The line was open, but silent. Someone was listening at the other end.

"Hello?"

There was a sound like someone smacking his lips.

"Who is this?"

The sound grew louder, and someone made a muffled growl. Laurie slammed the phone down and wrapped her arms around herself to keep from shaking.

The phone rang again. Laurie looked at it, debating. Then, after three rings, she picked it up and held it to her ear for a long moment before venturing to speak. "Hello?"

"Why'd you hang up on me?" Annie said indignantly, swallowing whatever she'd been chewing.

"Annie, was that you?" Laurie's fingertips flew to her bosom in relief.

"Of course."

"Why didn't you say anything? You scared me to death."

"I had my mouth full of peanut butter. Couldn't you hear me?"

"No."

"What did you think it was?"

"I don't know, an obscene phone call or something."

"Well, now you hear obscene chewing." And she smacked her lips and tongue around the remnant of the soggy sandwich. "You know, you're losing control, Laurie."

"I think I've already lost it."

"I doubt that. Listen, my mother is letting me use her car. I'll pick you up. Six thirty."

"Sure. See you later."

"Don't speak to any strange bogeymen—unless they're good dancers."

"Okay. 'Bye." She put the phone down and tried to do some homework, but the books lay on her desk as if written in some extraterrestrial script. Every subject she tried to study led her by free association to the phantom prowler who'd been dogging her footsteps all day long. The English lit homework on the theme of fate brought her mind back to poor Judith Myers, who'd met hers precisely fifteen years ago this very day— almost this very hour! She tried math, but all she could think of were all those stab wounds seeping crimson blood from Judith's brutally violated body. In history they were studying Julius Caesar's reign, and she'd just begun to get into it when she came across the passage about the emperor's assassination by Brutus and his friends—by daggers concealed beneath their togas.

She pushed her chair back violently, stood up, and began to pace around the room, pounding her fist in her palm. "Calm down, Laurie, this is ridiculous," she told herself aloud.

And it was. But she kept glancing out the window anyway.

9

The sky had turned a marble gray with storm clouds rolling in from the west, but the setting sun ignited them from underneath like an orange blowtorch, illuminating the polished marble gravestones of the Haddonfield Town Cemetery in a rare display of joyous glitter.

Angus Taylor, the caretaker of the nondenominational cemetery, puffed up the sharp incline, reading from a note pad as he led his trench coat-clad guest along a flagstone path. "Can't take this hill like I once used to," he said between anguished breaths. "Too much beer, not enough sex. Of course, I hold that a man can't have too much of either, but I suppose if I had my druthers it'd be . . ."

A glance at the visitor, who stared at him with a mixture of indifference or repugnance, subdued Taylor's chatter. He stopped a moment, panting, to look at the map on his note pad. "Let's see. Myers. Judith Myers. Row eighteen, plot twenty. Over this way."

They veered onto a secondary path whose stones had all but sunk beneath the encroaching grass. Willow branches whipped their faces as they peered through the impending gloom at names and dates that bespoke lives rich and inglorious, lives joyous and sad, lives short and long,

78

but all terminated inexorably by the same grim hand.

The garrulous Taylor waxed silent. Though he'd been in the undertaking business all his life, it wasn't until lately that he'd begun to realize that his interest had become more than professional. At the age of sixty-two, the dozens of graves whose excavation he supervised had begun to beckon to him, and he'd started to ponder what it meant to spend an eternity in one. He'd arranged to be baptized so that he could be buried in a churchyard, where at least there might be the illusion of grace and salvation, and where he'd be surrounded by people bound to him by their mutual faith. "You believe in God, mister?"

Sam Loomis studied the man from beneath craggy brows and decided it wasn't worth getting into a philosophical debate. "Doesn't everyone?" he said. "Which way?"

"Left."

They walked slowly, scanning the stones.

"Every town has something like this happen," the puffing man said. "I remember a guy over in Russellville, Charley Bowles? Nicest guy you could ever imagine. You could boot him in the tail, he'd never complain. Then, maybe some twenty years ago I recollect, he finished dinner, excused himself from the table, and went into the garage. Come back with a hacksaw, he did. Kissed the wife and two kids good-bye, then proceeded to . . ."

"Mr. Taylor, where are we?" Loomis snapped.

Taylor held his note pad up to catch the fading sunlight. "Just right over there a ways. And I remember Judith Myers. Talk about sweet girls. She'd bat her eyes at you, you wanted to melt through the floor. Of course, they did find traces of semen, and this fella did admit he'd been humpin' her a few hours before, but that doesn't make a girl a tramp. Not these days. I know of a *fourteen*-year-old who's been . . . *hmm.* I thought it was right about here." He consulted his pad and looked at a marble marker sunk into the ground at the convergence of two paths.

"Lost?" said Loomis with a sharp edge of exasperation.

"Should be right behind Ed Sanders and next to Cornelia Stirley. Aw, shit!"

They stepped up to the Judith Myers plot.

The stone was gone.

The earth had been exposed so recently, Loomis could smell the fresh loam and see long livid earthworms trailing into the ground after their violent disturbance.

"Goddamn kids. This happens to me every Halloween."

"You're sure it's Judith Myers?" Loomis's eyes glowed red in the direct glint of sunset.

"Here, see for yourself." Taylor held the note pad up for Loomis to read. Pointing a pudgy finger at the diagram, he said, "See? Seventeen, eighteen is Myers, nineteen is Cornelia Stirley. It's Judith Myers, no doubt about it. Stone should be lying around nearby, if you want to help me look for it. They usually get tired of trying to haul these things and give up."

"Who does?"

"The kids. Teenagers, college kids."

"What do they do with them?"

"Play pranks. Put them on people's lawns. One bunch two years ago put one in the principal's office at school. Ho, what a stink he made, whoo-boy!" Taylor took a few paces downhill, scanning the surrounding ground for the stone.

"You won't find it," Loomis announced calmly.

"What makes you so sure?"

"I'm sure. He's come home," Sam Loomis said, leaning heavily on a tombstone.

10

The trick-or-treaters were in full bloom. The children had poured out of their homes simultaneously, as if on some signal unheard by grown-ups. Laurie stood on the sidewalk outside her house, one eye cocked for Annie's red two-door hardtop, and watched the procession of pirates, clowns, cowboys, witches, skeletons, ballerinas, policemen, firemen, doctors, nurses, and soldiers that trooped up and down the block in clusters of four or five, methodically working the streets with their ever-fattening mass-produced orange-and-black shopping bags.

What touched her most deeply was the realization that these children were free and safe to roam the streets unhindered, unworried by the bullies and muggers and purse snatchers that lay in wait in the shadows of New York or Chicago or the other big cities. Oh, one or two knots of children were accompanied by an adult, but this was for traffic supervision, not protection against crime. The littlest ones tended to cross streets without looking at this dusky hour, where the all-but-settled sun glinted with a brightness equal to the orange jack-o'-lanterns that rested on porch railings or in windows in every house. Oh, one did read in the newspapers every year about some mad person who hated children and injected poison into apples or concealed razor blades in trick-

81

or-treat candy. But that wasn't why the occasional parent could be seen tagging along with a pack of beggar-children, looking foolish in grownup clothes or even more foolish in costume. No, there was no danger to the child who walked the sundown streets of Haddonfield.

At least not, Laurie pondered, from without. But from within? Was it not possible that among these dozens of gaily cavorting children there was one capable of a crime so heinous it made the gorge rise in your throat just to think about it? It would be ridiculous, laughable, had it not been so fifteen years ago this very night. They said he had on a clown costume, Laurie said, scanning the little revelers for a clown costume. She found four in the space of a minute. That one of them could produce a knife and ventilate her entrails was a thought far more horrifying than the thought of the same knife wielded by some city cutthroat, from whom you at least expected it. Laurie flashed for a second on Judith Myers and tried to put herself in Judy's place as the boy with the rosy cheeks and fawn eyes exposed the blade of his butcher knife and began to advance on her. It's a joke, you can stop now, Laurie heard herself telling her own imaginary kid brother. But the kid brother didn't stop, and when he brought the blade up and then down that first time, just before that point penetrated your flesh, you knew something about evil that had been forgotten for centuries, maybe millennia.

You knew in that instant that everything you had been brought up to believe, everything you had counted on for security, everything you took for granted as normal, all of it was a lie of such enormity that if you could live for another hundred years, let alone another five seconds, you could never fully grasp it. In that instant of frozen time between the downward thrust of the child's arm and the searing agony of his blade

plunging hotly into your body, your mind took
stock of everything that had meant comfort to
you; the television set and the air conditioner, the
late-model car with three hundred horsepower
and rack-and-pinion steering and disc brakes, the
refrigerator-freezer that made ice cubes, the elec-
tric range that signaled you when your roast was
ready, your gas heater that flicked on automatically when the temperature in your home dropped
below sixty-five degrees, the happy house and lov-
ing parents and terrific teachers and great
friends, you surveyed them all and they were lies,
lies, for when it came to shielding your belly from
this crazed six-year-old's right hand, these com-
forts were as thin as the silk panties that shielded
it now, for all the protection they rendered.

"Trick or treat!"

Laurie clutched her stomach involuntarily.
"Get away from me!" she screamed.

The children's eyes rounded, and they backed
away several steps.

Laurie caught her breath and laughed sheep-
ishly. "Oh, I'm sorry, you snuck up on me. This
is my house, here. Go up to the door, my mother
has some goodies for you."

Get a grip on yourself, Laurie said to herself
as the children traipsed up to her front door.

Annie's car whipped around the corner and
screeched to a stop. Laurie walked around to the
passenger side and got in. She sniffed the air. "Do
you have to smoke that stuff when you drive?"

"Well. excuuuuuuse me!"

"Look, I'm no prude, but there *are* kids all
over the place tonight, so drive carefully, huh?"

"Yes, Mommy," Annie said, pulling away
from the curb with exaggerated caution.

"Where are we going?"

"The usual. Just a cruise around town to see
who's hanging out, and with whom. Then on to
our babysitting assignments. Barf. And you ask

if I have to smoke," she said, groping around her purse and removing a clumsily rolled joint in canary yellow paper. At a stop sign she lit it, pulling on it with a hissing intake of air and offering it to Laurie.

Grass never did much for Laurie, and she didn't expect it to do much this time, but it was the social thing to do, so she dragged on it the way she'd been taught. She must have hit a hot spot in the joint, or perhaps it was a particularly rough weed, because she started to cough uncontrollably.

Annie took the joint back. "You'll never make a good dope addict," she said, hitting it again.

They drove casually in the general direction of town, Laurie holding in her lap the pumpkin she'd brought for Tommy Doyle. They passed a few friends, nobody special, so they honked and waved and drove on.

"You still spooked?" Annie asked her friend.

"I wasn't spooked."

"Lies."

"I saw someone standing in Mr. Riddle's backyard, that's all."

"Probably Mr. Riddle."

"He was watching me."

"Mr. Riddle was watching you?" Annie gave that three-note giggle she always seemed to utter when she was getting high. "Laurie, Mr. Riddle is eighty-seven."

"He can still watch."

"That's probably all he can do." Annie looked in her rearview mirror before hanging a left, and casually noted the same station wagon she'd shouted at after school. It was about fifty yards behind her. It was probably nothing, and not wanting to alarm Laurie more than the poor girl was already alarmed, Annie decided to say nothing. But she wondered who this El Creepo was. If you're trying to meet a couple of chicks, this sure wasn't the way to do it. And if you're some kind of pervert, tailing chicks through the streets of a small town is about as subtle as throwing a bomb into a police station.

She checked the rearview mirror again and he was gone. Too bad. Now she'd never know. But she had a thought by association, and she uttered it. "Have you ever worn a mask?"

"Huh?"

"When you wear a mask, like at Halloween? But I mean a really good one that disguises your face so that people really don't know who you are?"

"What about it?" Laurie's brow wrinkled as she waited for the punch line.

"I was just thinking, you can say or do anything from behind that mask, because people don't know who you are."

"It's like the *Alexandria Quartet*," said Laurie. "Lawrence Durrell?"

"I never read that."

"I'm sure," Laurie teased. "Somewhere in one of those novels Durrell describes the terrible things that happen on carnival night because people wear masks. Murders, rapes, people hiding behind the anonymity to take advantage of each other . . ."

"Oh, goody, can I get a student discount on a ticket to Alexandria?"

"Be serious, Annie, you're the one who started this conversation."

"Sorry. But see, that's just what I mean. The idea of not being responsible for anything I do because I'm wearing a mask—it's kind of arousing."

"For you, maybe. But then, you find everything arousing."

"Oh, well, that's the kind of girl I'm. Maybe you ought to put on a mask and let some of your inhibitions out, do something mad. It's

Halloween, what better time to raise a little hell? I'll bet that deep down in you there's a fiend who'd push little old ladies in front of cars if you thought you could get away with it."

"Never!" Laurie gasped. Then, pausing a beat as a sly smile spread over her face, "Little old men, maybe, but never little old ladies."

They burst into gales of laughter.

"What's the pumpkin for?" Annie said, tapping the object in her friend's lap.

"I brought it for Tommy. I figured that making a jack-o'-lantern would keep him occupied."

"I always said you'd make a fabulous girl scout."

"Thanks."

"For that matter, I might as well be a girl scout myself tonight," she sighed.

"Because you got shot down, you mean," Laurie said.

"Yeah. I guess we'll make popcorn and watch *Doctor Dementia*. Six straight hours of horror movies. Little Lindsey Wallace won't know what hit her."

"Better horror movies than the real thing," said Laurie wistfully.

Annie's brows furrowed. "Now, what is that supposed to mean?"

"Nothing, just some morbid thoughts I've been having today."

Annie offered her friend the half-smoked joint. "You'd better take a great big hit of this thing, honey. It's a sure cure for the morbids."

Laurie pushed it away. "Annie, do you ever think about, well, evil?"

"Uh-oh, it's serious time."

Laurie held her peace, forcing Annie to reflect.

"Well, you know, daddy's a cop, and he's told me some things. I don't know if you'd call them evil, exactly. We don't get much of it around here. We don't get much of anything around here! But when he worked in Columbus? He saw some pretty heavy things go down: beatings, rapes, murders. Sounded evil enough to me. Anyway, I try not to think about stuff like that. Whenever I do, I switch the channel . . ."

"I wish I could turn my mind off as easily as you," Laurie lamented.

"It's easy when you don't have that much of a mind to begin with. Hey, talk about my father!" As the car bore around a gentle curving approach to town, they saw the sheriff's car parked outside Nichols's Hardware Store. The car's revolving red and blue lights and flashers illuminated the hardware, candy, and liquor stores adjoining it as darkness began to descend on Haddonfield. An alarm bell rang shrilly, and a knot of onlookers stared at Annie's father as he stood in front of the broken plate glass window examining the damage.

Annie and Laurie hastily rolled their windows down and waved their hands like frightened birds to chase the cloying smoke smell out of the car. Annie noticed the station wagon that had been following them peel off down Main Street as she pulled her car over to the curb. Lee Brackett brightened and ambled over to the car. "Hi, Annie, Laurie."

"Hi, Dad. What happened?"

"Huh?" He pointed at the hardware store and Annie realized the man hadn't heard her over the clangor of the alarm bell. She repeated her question louder. "Someone broke into the hardware store. Probably kids."

"You blame everything on kids," Annie rejoined.

He shrugged. "The only things missing were some Halloween masks, rope, and a set of carving knives, as far as Mr. Nichols has been able to figure. What does that sound like to you, a middle management executive for IBM?"

Annie looked at her friend. "It's hard growing up with a cynic."

"Don't you have a babysitting job, sweetheart?" her father shouted.

"What?"

"I said, 'Don't you have a babysitting job?' You're going to be late!"

"He shouts too," Annie said, waving at her father. The girls rolled up their windows and laughed.

"Do you think he smelled anything?" Laurie asked, testing the air with her nostrils.

"My father? He's a good cop, but he's a lousy detective."

"I hope so. I'd hate for it to get back to my folks."

"Listen, Laurie, if your parents don't know you smoke grass, they probably haven't noticed you've grown boobs, either." She glanced sidelong at Laurie's chest. "I take that back. I'm not sure anybody's noticed you've grown boobs."

"Damn daughter's been smoking whoopee-weed again," Sheriff Brackett muttered to himself as he observed a dour-looking, bald man with a gray goatee stepping out of the crowd. The man wore a chocolate-colored suit beneath a rumpled trench coat.

"Sheriff? I'm Dr. Sam Loomis," the man shouted over the alarm.

"Lee Brackett," the sheriff said, looking at him critically. "We don't need a doctor. It's just a routine break-in."

"I'm not that kind of doctor. I'd like to talk with you, if I could."

"It may be a few minutes. I gotta stick around here."

"It's important." His eyes, sunken and slightly red-rimmed, appealed to Brackett like a hound's at the dinner table.

Brackett looked at his watch and shrugged. "Ten minutes?"

"I'll be here," Loomis said, turning just a moment too late to notice the station wagon he'd been hunting pull away after its occupant had stopped to observe him.

Brackett didn't see it either. He had heard the call come over the radio last night and this morning, and though nobody had fully explained who was supposed to be driving the liver-colored station wagon with the state emblem on the doors, he'd have chased it down routinely.

Loomis killed the ten minutes with a stroll down Main Street, looking indifferently into windows of stores and shops that were interchangeable with those of any town this size in the Midwest. There were a few signs of changing times, such as an organic health food shop, a bookstore with a surprisingly intellectual selection of titles in the window, and a coffee shop specializing in espresso, capuccino, and herb teas, a far cry from the usual Midwest coffee shop purveying the kind of diner fare that truckdrivers thrived on. But at least there was no head shop, as one commonly saw in the bigger midwestern towns and cities: no shop selling cigarette papers, pipes, coke spoons and the more exotic paraphernalia of the dope trade. Though Loomis knew that the kids used drugs in these towns, the town governments came down very hard on any overt display of drug cultures.

As Loomis passed a liquor store, he nodded, remembering his teenage son's recent tirade about the hypocrisy of Loomis's generation that punishes drug use but proudly displays its alcoholic orientation as if drinking were a virtue to be encouraged. The boy was right. But it would be another decade before you saw a head shop in Haddonfield, Illinois.

Brackett was just finishing writing up his report and supervising the hasty assembly of a saw-horse barrier around the hardware store. Mr. Nichols put the finishing touches on a wooden panel to cover the broken window until a glass replacement arrived in the morning. He stepped back to survey his handiwork and examine the rim of the window as if to contemplate the possibility of putting up a locked iron gate. He shook his head sadly. He hated to do that. To put up a gate would not only be ugly, it would symbolize his concession to the growing vandalism that existed in his town.

"May we sit in your car, Sheriff?" Loomis asked.

"Suit yourself, Doctor." They slid into the front seat. Brackett turned the heater on. "Getting a bit chilly. Winter'll be here any day now."

"*Mmm*," Loomis said distractedly, running his fingers down the blue barrels of the sheriff's over-and-under twelve-gauge shotgun propped vertically between the seats. "Have you ever had to use this thing?"

"Can't catch quail with my bare hands," Brackett laughed.

"You know what I mean."

Brackett shook his head. "I've pointed it at one or two 'alleged perpetrators,' as my colleagues like to call them."

"Who do you think perpetrated *that*?" Loomis asked with a jerk of the head toward the hardware store.

"Kids, most likely. Who else would steal Halloween masks?"

"And knives? And rope? What do kids need with those?"

"Beats the hell out of *me*. Sometimes they break in and grab whatever's near to hand, just

because it's there for the grabbing." He gazed at
Loomis, whose face glowed green in the phos-
phorescent light of the dashboard. "You got any
better ideas?"

"I might. Do you remember the Judith Myers
case?"

Brackett's gaze narrowed to a suspicious
stare. "Of course I do." There was a silence as
Loomis ran his fingers with a scratchy noise
through his goatee. Brackett waited impatiently,
studying this man whose intrusion into his life
had brought with it intimations of grisly horror,
a horror made more dreadful because it had happened in this idyllic setting. Over the police channel, staticky squawks proclaimed petty vandalism
occurring throughout the area. "Intruders reported on Carter Road around the Gleason farm";
"windows broken by four persons in masks, believed children, Carty house at Post Road near
Deller"; "three trespassers reported writing on
doors with spray paint . . ."

"What are you saying, Doctor?"

Loomis told him about the escape from the
sanitarium last night. Brackett listened with a
troubled expression. "The Myers house. Will you
take me there?"

Brackett tapped the steering wheel with his
nails. "I don't know, Loomis. I got my hands full
tonight. Halloween is one of my profession's busy
seasons. Can you hear what's coming down?" He
turned the radio louder.

Loomis listened stolidly, expressionlessly.
"This is all the work of children!" he protested at
length. "Harmless pranks!"

"Do you call broken windows and spray-
painted doors harmless? Try repairing them some-
time. Try paying for them. Across the country
the damages amount to *millions. Millions!*"

"But we're talking about something else,
Sheriff, another . . . another *dimension*."

"I don't know about other dimensions, Loomis, but I do know that the harm being rendered by your so-called sweet innocent children tonight is more real to me than something perpetrated by a nut case fifteen years ago."

"An *escaped* nut case."

Loomis's distinction made a telling point on the sheriff. "*Umm*, that's true," he conceded reluctantly.

Loomis drove the point home. "Do you think this man has come here to soap people's windows?" He rubbed his goatee heavily, until it sounded like a carpenter sandpapering a table.

Brackett shrugged. "I suppose it's worth a look, but I guarantee you're not going to find anything."

"That, Sheriff, is a guarantee I would too gladly accept."

Another squawk came over the radio. "Fire reported in meadow behind Kochner farm, route 167-A off Market Road," the voice droned.

"Kids will be kids," the sheriff laughed bitterly.

Loomis still wasn't sure Brackett had grasped the problem.

As Brackett nosed his car into the dark, cloudy night, he reviewed for Loomis everything he knew or had heard about the Myers case. Loomis listened attentively, though from his half-closed lids Brackett might have concluded the man was dozing off. Brackett said nothing Loomis didn't know, until something slipped out casually that made the psychiatrist's eyes widen and his back stiffen. "Would you mind repeating that, Sheriff?"

"I said, the kid's great-grandfather had done something similar."

"Tell me about it." Loomis was breathing harder. Brackett's casual remark had excited him as if he were a starving man that someone had dangled a piece of cake in front of.

"Well, I don't know much about it, and it was never brought out in the hearings, but Mrs. Myers, that night, was overheard saying, 'He's come back,' or maybe 'It's come back.' Over and over again. I didn't live here then, so this is all second-hand."

"Go on."

"So Ron Barstow, he was sheriff at the time, Ron asked her, 'Who's come back? What's come back?' And she mumbled something about the thing that had got inside her grandfather. I guess she meant taken possession."

Despite the coldness of the evening, Loomis had begun to perspire. His breath hissed noisily. "Did she explain, about the thing that had taken possession of her grandfather?"

"No, but Ron went to the records at town hall and checked out the newspaper clippings at the historical society."

"And?"

"It seems the man had gone berserk back in the eighteen nineties."

Loomis was on the edge of his seat, his eyes bulging. "Berserk? How?"

"It was at a Grange dance, I think Ron said. The man just upped and pulled a revolver from his belt and blasted a dancing couple. They hanged him."

They drove silently for a moment, Loomis struggling to contain his excitement, almost savoring the next question. "When did this happen?"

"Eighteen ninety-eight, ninety-nine, something like that."

"No, no, I mean, what date?"

"How should I . . . ? Wait a minute. Of course I know! Ron remarked on it."

"Yes?"

"All Hallow Even. It was a harvest dance. Halloween!" Brackett's toe unconsciously depressed the gas pedal and the car accelerated into the dangerous night. "Jesus," the sheriff breathed.

"Why wasn't this mentioned at the hearing?" Loomis demanded, slumping back into his seat, still panting.

"I think Ron said it was because the defense attorney thought it was either irrelevant or damaging to the kid's case."

"Irrelevant? Damaging?" Loomis chuckled drily, a laugh totally devoid of humor, like a rattle. "Tell me, did your friend tell you anything more about this great-grandfather?"

"I'm thinking." The seconds ticked ponderously around the clock on the dashboard. "Voices."

"Voices?"

"The man heard voices, voices telling him to kill these two."

"Kill those two specifically. In other words, he didn't fire into a crowd at random? He knew the victims?"

Brackett scratched his ear. "I'm a little confused about that part. The way Ron explained it, the guy *claimed* he knew who he was shooting, but when they asked him to identify his victims, he called them some weird names he said he'd heard in his dreams." Brackett pointed to his own skull and made a rotary motion with his finger. "Crazy."

"Perhaps. These names, Sheriff. Were they Celtic? Would you recognize them? Deirdre? Cullain?"

"Sorry, my friend, they don't ring a bell. Who are they?"

"Names of victims in Michael's dreams. If

we could establish a continuity from the great-grandfather to the boy . . ." the psychiatrist mused.

"A continuity?" Brackett gasped. "Come on, Loomis. In order for a dream to jump two or three generations, you'd have to believe . . ." He shook his head. "Doctor, I think you may be touched yourself."

"Probably. It's an occupational hazard."

Brackett swung right and glided to the curb before the gloomy, weatherbeaten house that stood out among its white, neatly kempt neighbors like some shriveled crone in a row of teenagers. They climbed out of the car and stood before it, listening to the sound of branches whipping against an upstairs window. "Has anybody lived here since . . . ?"

"You got to be kidding," Brackett said. "Every kid in Haddonfield thinks the place is haunted. Maybe every adult too."

"They may be right."

Brackett reached into his car and produced a long flashlight. Pointing it at the "For Sale" sign thrust into the scrubby lawn, the sheriff said, "His parents found him standing right there in his clown costume with the ruff around the neck, cute as could be except he held a butcher knife as long as this flashlight and he was smeared with fresh blood." He flashed his light on the sign. "This should come down. I hear it's been sold. Chester Strode must be drunk with relief. He's the agent."

"Sold?" Loomis repeated, shaking his head with disbelief.

"I know what you mean. New York people. They thought it would be fun to own a haunted house. New Yorkers," he groaned, using the word almost as a curse.

"Can we go in?"

"I don't have a key, but maybe . . ." They mounted the front porch.

"We could go in through one of the broken windows," Loomis suggested.

"That's what I was going to sug——*hmm.*"

Loomis stepped to the front door, on which the sheriff held his light. The knob dangled at an odd angle, and there were fresh gouges in the wood around it. Brackett touched the knob and the door swung open. "One haunted house, complete with creaks," he said.

"If you find it so amusing, why are you taking your gun out of its holster?" Loomis asked with a grim smile.

Brackett didn't care for the remark. Flashing the light around the entry vestibule, he stepped in cautiously, crouched tensely as he scanned the rooms with his light-guided eyes, then gestured with his head for Loomis to come in. Carefully they trod the floorboards, Loomis moving back to back with his friend, like a pair of eyes in the back of the sheriff's head. The psychiatrist kept his right hand plunged deep in the pocket of his trench coat.

Suddenly Brackett stopped. Loomis backed into him. "What is it?"

Brackett trained his light on a corner of the parlor next to the kitchen. "That's a good question. What *is* it?"

The light revealed something resembling a white and black shaggy throw rug with jagged red streaks. Brackett kneeled over it and gulped. "It's a dog." He reached out and dipped a finger into the entrails that had been ripped out of the creature and draped across its hind legs casually. "Still warm. Lord!"

Loomis looked at the mutilated creature, its bulging eyes orangely reflecting the light. "He got hungry."

"He? You mean . . . ? Come on, Doctor. It could have been a skunk. Or a raccoon."

"Could have been," Loomis said unenthusiastically.

"A man wouldn't do that," Brackett said, holding the light on the glistening guts.

"He isn't a man," Loomis replied.

They turned their back on the remains and searched the rest of the downstairs. The place was a shambles. Floorboards ripped up, plaster and lathing chipped or ripped off the walls, damp spots in the ceiling. Brackett made several more sarcastic remarks about the people from New York.

"Shall we go upstairs?" Loomis said.

"Uh, of course. What tour of a haunted house would be complete without a look at the upstairs?"

"After you, Sheriff."

Brackett snorted and stepped ahead of Loomis. They inched up the stairs, staying close to the wall, for the balustrade was a wreck. As they approached the landing, Brackett paused and caught his breath. "What do you suppose that noise is?"

Loomis cocked his ear. "I believe it's a branch slapping a window. It's coming from that room there. I saw it when we were on the lawn."

"Of course," Brackett said, crunching over some plaster pebbles.

Holding gun and flashlight close together, he stepped into the near bedroom. The noise was indeed what Loomis had said. "This is where it happened. She was sitting there, brushing her hair. I'm told she just had panties on. He came in here, and of course she recognized him and did nothing to defend herself. Why should she? It was her six-year-old kid brother, for crying out loud! They found her here, under this . . ." A sudden gust of wind slapped the branch against the window with terrible force, smashing it and showering glass at their feet. Both men leaped back, uttering curses. Then they laughed nervously.

Brackett led Loomis through the rest of the upstairs at double time, then said, "Nothing here. Let's go."

Outside, Brackett leaned against his car. "What do we do?"

"He was here and he may be coming back. I'm going to wait for him."

"I keep thinking I should call in help, maybe get a warning broadcast."

"If you do, people will see him everywhere, on every street corner, in every house. Just tell your men to shut their mouths and open their eyes."

The sheriff gestured at his shotgun. "You want something?"

"I've got something." Loomis pulled a .357 magnum out of his raincoat. Brackett whistled. It looked like a naval gun. "Don't worry. It's licensed."

"Lord. You're loaded for bear."

11

He kept his headlights off as he followed the red car with the two girls in it, and he kept his distance. His heart beat heavily but rhythmically, but the beat had accelerated since sundown, and it was beginning to make him nervous and agitated. His palms were sweaty and his mouth dry, and he was uncomfortably aroused, a condition of pain and not pleasure. He drove past the orange-glowing pumpkin-faces that seemed to mock him, past the eager, laughing children parading from house to house in their foolish costumes.

He remembered the clown suit he had worn that night, red and green with a lace ruff and a sock cap with a silly ball at the end of it that kept dangling in front of his nose. He remembered his grandmother's smell as she took a tuck in the material of his costume. He remembered the taste of candy corn at the party that evening, remembered biting off the white tips of the pyramid-shaped candies, then the orange middle, then the yellow bottom, trying to determine if they were made of different-tasting stuff but they were the same candy dyed three different colors.

He remembered too how, in the middle of it, in the middle of ducking for apples, the feeling had come over him, a force like an iron hand that

99

virtually shoved him out of the door and into the street, his little legs carrying him home and a voice telling him what he had to do. In his mind's eye he had seen, that night, a picture of his sister as he had seen it a few times through the keyhole of her bedroom or in the crack of the bathroom door, pink, firm, with beautiful tight buttocks and round high breasts with jutting nipples, and the voice told him he must carve those breasts and buttocks into a thousand slabs of bloody meat. He remembered his own internal voice protesting, but it was such a helpless little-boy voice that the grown-up voice had shouted it down easily and urged his little legs home faster, instructing him to go into the house through the kitchen door, remove the butcher knife from the drawer under the sink, and go upstairs.

He remembered the look in her eyes as he entered her room, a look that darkened from surprise to recognition to horror in the space of a second. He remembered the little-boy voice crying *What are you doing?* but the grown-up voice crying *Stick it in her belly! Stick it in her heart! Stick it in her face! Stick it in her arms. Stick it in her legs! Stab her! Cut her! Slice her! Slash her!* KILL HER! KILL HER! KILL HER! KILL HER! KILL HER! KILL HER! KILL HER! KILL HER!

He had known she was screaming because he saw her lips moving but he heard nothing but the roar of the grown-up voice in his ears. He remembered the heat of her blood as it splashed his hands, and the strangely familiar smell of it.

He remembered looking at her almost unrecognizable remains on the floor and hearing the little-boy voice saying, *Uh-oh, you're gonna get in a lot of trouble when mommy and daddy get home.* And that's just what happened.

Mommy and daddy were very mad at him when they came home.

And now the voice was talking to him again, and it was almost the same way except that he was a grown-up himself now, and he was as big and strong as his daddy, and this time nobody would be able to take him away and send him someplace.

The brake lights of the car in front of him went on, and he hit his own brakes, drifting to the side of the road to watch. The blond girl got out, the one who had come up to the door of his home this morning, the one who reminded him so much of Judy. He watched her go up to the white house and ring the doorbell while her friend turned into the driveway of the large house across the street and pull into a garage.

The door opened for the blond girl, and she stepped inside. Then, across the street, the dark-haired girl emerged from the garage, rang the doorbell, and was admitted.

He watched.

Five minutes later, a man and a woman came out of each house. The man and woman coming out of the house where the blonde had gone kissed a little boy good-bye. The man and woman coming out of the house where the dark-haired girl had gone kissed a little girl good-bye. Then each couple got into a car. They went off in different directions.

He got out of the station wagon and slid into the hedgerows around the house with the blonde and the little boy in it, the dark uniform he'd taken off the driver blending with the night shadows. He sidled up to a window. Beyond it was a darkened room, but through an open door at the other end he could see the girl who reminded him of Judy talking to the boy. The boy was almost as young as he'd been fifteen years ago. The boy was wearing a shiny jump suit with astronaut patches on it. This was the boy he'd seen bullied at school today.

He walked around the house, silently testing windows and doors, noting that a pair of French windows outside the television room were open, but not venturing in yet. Not yet.

He drifted back to the front of the house and pressed against the hedges as a gaggle of children passed by, close enough for him to grab. It was too dangerous.

When it was safe, he ventured across the street. The house was enormous, with a large porch n two sides. Again, he walked around it, looking in the windows. He saw the dark-haired girl standing before a hall mirror, brushing out her hair and chatting to the little girl who watched her admiringly. The dark-haired girl had big breasts that jutted out even with her arms stretched overhead.

He stalked like a cat to the side and back of the house, noting an unlocked kitchen door. In the backyard, a slate path led to a little house like a bungalow. He went up to it and peered inside. It had a washer and dryer.

He returned to the main house and watched some more. The sex between his legs throbbed in an unpleasant way. The voice was whispering something to him that he couldn't make out yet, but he knew that if he waited it would get louder.

In his belt were the carving knife and rope he had taken from the store in town.

"Well, what shall we do?" Laurie said, looking at her watch. She knew the answer, but hoped against hope that Tommy Doyle would suggest that he play a quiet game by himself while she studied history. Sure!

Tommy pointed to the stack of comic books

in the den. "We can start with those. When we're finished, I have some more in my room."

"And what happens when we finish those?" Laurie said sarcastically.

"Well, I have a big stack of old ones in my closet," he answered solemnly.

"I thought you might," she sighed.

They sat down in a small sofa, and Laurie took a comic book off the top of the stack. " 'How now,' cried Arthur . . ."

"What does it mean, he cried? Why is he crying?"

"He's not crying-crying, Tommy. A cry also means a shout. 'How now,' *cried* Arthur. 'Then none may pass this way without a fight?' 'Just so,' answered the knight in a bold and haughty manner . . ." She rattled the comic book. "Stop squirming. What's the matter?"

"I don't like that story."

"I thought King Arthur was your favorite?"

"Not anymore. Can you keep a secret?"

"Sure."

He fell to his hands and knees and reached under the sofa, producing another stack of comics.

"Why are they under there?"

"Mom doesn't like me to have them."

Laurie shuffled through them. "Neutron Man, Laser Man, Tarantula Man . . . I can see why."

"I think they're neat."

"Neat," Laurie echoed weakly.

"Laurie, is there really a bogeyman?"

"Of course. He eats little boys who read comic books."

"Really?" The boy's eyes widened. "Maybe I'll watch TV the rest of the night."

"That would suit . . . there's the phone." She crossed the room to the phone on a table near the opposite sofa, a tremor of nervousness vibrating through her stomach . . . "Hello?"

Her anxiety wasn't helped by the noise on the other end of the line. It sounded like gunfire. Finally, a voice. "Hear that? That's the sound of popping corn. That's the sound of a horny teenage girl when her boyfriend's shot her down," Annie said, bored.

"My heart bleeds for you."

"Are you having fun? Never mind, I'm sure you are. I have big, big news for you."

"What is it?"

"Well . . . *oops!* Hold on a minute."

Laurie listened to the noise on the other end of the line with growing alarm. "Ow! Hey, cut it out . . . C'mon, get out of here . . . Jesus, that hurt, you big jerk . . . Lindsey! Lindsey, he's tearing me apart!"

"Annie!" Laurie yelled into the phone, her heart racing. "Annie, what's happening?"

"Lester is tearing my crotch out!" Annie shrieked. *"Lindsey! Get this goddamn dog out of here!"*

Laurie heard growling, scratching of nails on linoleum, then a little girl's voice. "Lester, c'mon, c'mon boy."

Annie came back on the phone, panting. "I hate that dog. I'm the only person in the world he doesn't like."

"It sounds like he likes you a lot," Laurie laughed.

"Nah, he's just a male. Goes for the crotch every time. Well, that's probably the only action I'm gonna see tonight, so maybe I shouldn't knock it."

"Annie, you are too gross for words. So what's this big, big news?"

"Would you believe you're going to the homecoming dance tomorrow night?"

"Not only wouldn't I believe it," Laurie said, "I'd say you must have the wrong number."

"That just goes to show how little *you* know."

"Oh? And what do *you* know?"

"Well, I just talked with Ben Tramer? And he got real excited when I told him how attracted to him you were."

Laurie's knees turned to rubber. "Oh, Annie, you didn't. Tell me you didn't."

"You guys will make a fabulous couple."

While the girls talked on the phone, Tommy Doyle looked out of the window at the last group of trick-or-treaters scurrying home in the darkness. His eyes were suddenly drawn to a black shape on the lawn across the street. For a second he thought it was one of those cardboard skeletons with moveable arms and legs that Lindsey's parents had hung from the tree. No, it was too big, too three-dimensional. It stood there, gazing at his house, gazing directly at *him*, not moving but definitely a living human, definitely not cardboard. Tommy gulped and turned away.

Laurie was still on the phone. Tommy tugged on her shirttail. "Laurie?"

"I'm so embarrassed," Laurie was saying. "I couldn't face him. I don't know if I could ever go back to school, I'm so embarrassed."

"You'll have to," Annie said. "He's calling you tomorrow to find out what time to pick you up."

"Annie, no. How could . . . hold on." She responded to the tug on her shirttail. "Tommy, I'm in the middle of a really important call."

"I know, but Laurie, the bogeyman is outside. C'mere and look."

"Don't go away, Annie, I have to check out the bogeyman."

"Ask him if he feels like getting laid," Annie said.

Laurie crossed to the window where Tommy stood holding the curtains apart. "There's nobody there, Tommy."

"There was."

"I'm sure. How about going into the living room and watching some TV? There's a whole bunch of horror movies on."

She turned away as Tommy remained at the window, peering into the night. The figure reappeared across the street and drifted toward the Wallace's kitchen window.

"False alarm," Laurie said.

"Too bad. It might have been different."

"Annie, some day you're going to get into big trouble."

"I can't wait. Anyway, look, it's simple. You like him, he likes you. All you need is a little push."

"I'd like to give *you* a little push, off the top of a building."

"It won't hurt you to go out with him, for God's sake. He's not exactly ... shit!"

"I know he's not exactly ..."

"No, I mean, I just spilled melted butter all over myself. I gotta call you back. I just made a mess of myself, as usual. Stand by." Laurie heard the sharp click and laughed. Annie was crazy, but she loved her. In fact, she loved her because she was crazy. Underneath the craziness was a warm person and a wonderful friend. Like this Ben Tramer thing. Sure it was presumptuous of Annie to tell Ben that Laurie liked him, but maybe it was all for the best. If Laurie wasn't capable of expressing herself to boys, how were they ever going to ask her out? In this day and age, girls were far more forward than ever before. The double standard was falling daily. Maybe Laurie would never be able to go as far as some of her friends—like Linda, whom Laurie had seen go up to a perfectly strange guy at a bar and say she'd like to ball him—but at least she could go further in that direction than she did now. And if not, she had Annie doing it for her. It was still horribly embarrassing, but heck, it wouldn't be the worst thing in the world, exactly, to get a phone call from Ben Tramer.

He stood watching the girl talk on the telephone. With her dark, curly hair and large breasts, she was not like Judy at all, but that was all right. They didn't have to look like Judy. They didn't even have to be girls.

She held the kitchen wall telephone tucked under her chin while she shook a large pot of popcorn over one burner of the stove with one hand and stirred a saucepan of butter with the other. Through the glass panels of the kitchen door he could hear her peculiar laughter.

Suddenly the big German shepherd dog came into the kitchen as she was starting to pour the butter over the popcorn. It startled her, and the butter splashed over her red sweater and plaid skirt. Her curse came sharply through the glass.

She hung up the phone and pulled the sweater over her head. She reached into a high shelf in the pantry to pull down a box of cornstarch. She dashed it on the butter stain on the sweater, then stepped out of her skirt and sprinkled the white powder on it too. She wore pink and blue print cotton panties bikini-style, and though her legs weren't as long as Judy's, her buttocks were larger and filled the pants to straining, and she had a sensual bulge just over her crotch that made him breathe heavily with desire. His hand opened and closed involuntarily on the handle of his knife.

She turned to face the door for a moment and he ducked back into the shadows. His head collided with a hanging plant, knocking the pot against the side of the house. He reached up to stay it but it was too late. The German shepherd began barking madly, the half-naked girl gave a startled scream, and the little girl started shouting at the dog to shut up.

The kitchen door opened and the girl,

clutching an apron to her breasts, peered out. He had melted back around the corner of the house and stood pinned to the wall, breathing noisily, knife poised. The dog's barking filled the night air with threats.

At length the girl uttered something about it having been the wind and closed the door. He could still hear the muffled baritone of the dog. He remained pinned to the wall, waiting for the barking to die down, but it went on ceaselessly. The dog knew he was there.

Suddenly the kitchen door opened again. "Lindsey," he heard the girl say, "Lester's driving me crazy. I'm going to let him out, okay?" An instant later the dog roared out of the house, clamoring and pacing the yard in a jerky search pattern as his nose picked up the confusing scents of the intruder's path. He crouched beside a rhododendron bush, braced for the leap he knew would come.

And come it did. The dog seemed to find the fresh scent and make his move in one fluid motion, emitting a chilling snarl as it arched through the air with bared fangs focused on the man's arms. But the man was prepared. Displaying a quickness and strength that some might have called supernatural, he dodged the charge and grabbed the dog from behind, clamping its jaws shut with one forearm and crushing its body to his chest with the other. The dog snarled and dug at his arms with the claws of its hind legs, but with its fangs ineffective it could do no serious harm. He clutched the dog tighter, his cablelike forearm closing its windpipe, his other arm pressing its spine against his ironlike ribs until he heard the satisfying crunch of shattering vertebrae. The dog emitted shrill squeals that subsided into puppyish whimpers as the life drained out of it. Its hind legs clawed feebly and futilely at his arms, then twitched several seconds more before going completely limp.

He held it a minute longer, then, certain it was dead, he dropped it into the rhododendron bush like a sackful of meat.

"Lester? Lester!" Annie's voice filled the night and was joined by the reedy voice of the little girl.

"What do you suppose happened to him?" the little one asked.

"I suppose he found a hot date, the lucky dog."

"What's a hot date, Annie?" he heard the kid ask as the doors closed again. He did not hear Annie's answer.

12

"Where's your laundry room?" Annie asked. She'd donned one of Mrs. Wallace's robes and stood before Lindsey, who was propped in a sofa before the television set, eyes fixed hypnotically on the opening credits of *The Thing*.

"Lindsey, did you hear me?"

The child was in a video trance.

"Earth to Lindsey, Earth to Lindsey, do you read me?" She stepped in front of the child, blocking her view of the set.

"Huh?"

"Where's your washing machine?"

"Outside."

"Outside," Annie mused. "I see. And I guess the dryer is in a tree."

"No, they're both outside in the little house in the yard."

"Why, may I ask?"

"Mommy didn't like the noise."

"Uh-huh. And she liked the inconvenience, I suppose?"

The kid shrugged her shoulders and pushed Annie out of the way. "I can't see the movie."

"I'm teddibly teddibly soddy," Annie said in her best British accent. "Okay, I'm going to carry this stuff out to the laundry house or whatever you call it. Will you be all right alone?"

The child gazed at the television set, unseeing

110

and unhearing except for what was emitted from the flickering tube.

"Jeez," said Annie, shaking her head. "And I thought *religion* was the opiate of the people." She stepped between Lindsey and the television set again. "I'll be back in five minutes after I put this in the washer, okay?"

"Uh," Lindsey said, straining to see the program around Annie's legs.

"I can't believe this," Annie muttered aloud as she crossed the flagstones to the little cottage in the backyard. A gust of wind whipped through the folds of her thin robe and blew it open. Annie's "Goddamn it!" echoed across the yard.

Freeing one hand from the load of laundry and the box of soap, she opened the door and stepped inside, dropping everything on the flat top of the dryer. She reached for the light switch that should have been placed just inside the door, but the Wallace family seemed to function on a logic all its own, for there was no switch there. "Terrific."

The door slammed shut.

Annie's heart leaped through her ribcage. She put her shoulder to it and with difficulty managed to open it, then turned her back to resume her search for the light switch. As she did, a face loomed outside the door, its rubbery features made more ghastly by the moonlight that made its sunken eyes and large nostrils absolutely black. The intruder's hand reached for the doorknob as he stared at the robed figure blindly groping for the light switch. Suddenly she found it and flicked the lights on. He jumped back into the cover of darkness, crunching the brittle dead leaves of another rhododendron.

The girl's head peered out. "Hello?" Silence. "Who's there?" More silence. "Paul? Is this one of your cheap tricks?" Silence again, save the soughing of the wind through the leaves of the trees. "I guess not," she said, disappointed. "No tricks for Annie tonight." She studied the dials on the washer, talking to herself to keep her jittery nerves under control. "Let's see, place the clothes inside, that I can do pretty well. Add soap or detergent, got it. Add fabric softener or bluing in reservoir where indicated, fuck that. Close door, turn left-hand dial to cold, warm, or hot, I think I'll do warm to melt the butter. Flip switch to small, medium, or large load, let's call it small. Jesus, they ought to give a course in laundry at school. Turn right-hand dial to wash, select number of minutes. Well, Annie, how does eight minutes sound to you. Wonderful. Pull dial out and get the fuck out of there."

The washing machine kicked into action as water poured into the drum.

Slam!

A tremendous gust of wind blew the door shut with window-rattling force. Annie rushed to the door and pulled the knob. The door didn't budge. She shook the door with adrenaline-triggered might, but even that didn't budge it. "Lindsey! *Lindsey!* Come out here! Sure she'll come out here. She wouldn't pull away from the television set if a nuclear missile scored a direct hit outside her house. Lindsey, Goddamn it, I'm stuck in the laundry!" She pounded the glass panes of the door, tempted to smash them, but decided instead to try the window over the dryer and spare herself the hassle of explaining and repaying the Wallaces for the damage.

She boosted herself up on top of the dryer and opened the window. It was small and she gauged its width against the size of her hips and decided it was going to be a near thing. But what else could she do?

She tried going out legs first, but her hips jammed and she decided they'd slide out better if she went out head first. As she pulled her breasts through the window frame she heard a phone ringing in the main house. "Oh, great," she moaned.

She also heard a sound in the hedges. It was not the wind. Her pelvis jerked forward in fright and her hips wedged tightly in the window frame. She heard a second sound, louder. Something was lurking in the bushes around the corner of the little house. It was closing in on her. "Lindsey! Lindsey! Oh God, *Lindsey* . . ."

"Annie?" Lindsey's voice tinkled on the windy night air. The thing in the bushes, whatever it was, retreated into the shadows as the little girl emerged from the darkness around the main house. "Annie, what are you doing?"

"What am I doing? I'm trying to widen this window with my hips, that's what I'm doing."

"It looks like you're stuck."

"I . . ." Annie drew a deep breath and overcame her fury. "Look, just try to open the door. Then pull me back inside, okay?"

"Okay."

Annie heard the rattling of the glass panes as Lindsey shook the door unsuccessfully. Then apparently the child put all of her strength into the effort, and Annie heard the satisfying surrender of the door and felt the cold night air on her feet. The next thing she knew, a pair of little hands was tugging her legs, and Annie got the leverage to twist her hips out of the window frame. She pulled her torso back into the laundry room and jumped down.

"Thank you, Lindsey. What made you come out here?"

"It was a commercial. And Paul called you. He's waiting on the phone."

"Paul? Paul is on the phone? Oh, God. Uh, Lindsey, run back up there and tell him I'll be right with him. And don't say anything about my getting stuck in here, okay?"

"Okay." Lindsey tramped down the flagstone path while Annie hastily transferred the wet laundry to the dryer, setting it for a half hour. Then she gathered her robe around her and raced across the yard, arriving just in time to hear Lindsey say into the phone, "She was stuck in the window, she'll be right here." She put the phone down and returned to her precious horror program.

"Hello, Paul."

"Hi, Annie. Listen, next time you want to leave the house, try this new invention I just heard about, much better than windows. It's called a door."

"All right, cut it out. I got stuck because your wonderful invention the door slammed behind me and I couldn't get it open. It can happen to anyone."

"Anyone with *your* figure."

"Yeah, well, I've seen you stuck in other positions!"

"Okay, okay. Now, here's the good news. My folks accepted a last-minute invitation to a party. They've just left."

"Well, to borrow a phrase from Linda, that's totally fantastic. Why don't you just walk over?"

"I have to stick around here. My parents said they'd call in just to check up on me. Can you believe that? So how about you coming here?"

"How can I? I'm sitting for Lindsey, remember?"

"Yeah." There was a pause as Paul thought it through. "Maybe you could drop Lindsey off with Laurie. She's sitting right across the street, right?"

"Not a bad idea. But my clothes are in the wash. I can't come now."

"Come without them."

"Shut up, jerk. I've got a robe on. That's all you think about."

"And you don't?"

"That's not true. I think about lots of things." A sly grin brightened her face. "Why don't we not stand here talking about them and get down to doing them? All right, see you in a few minutes." She hung up the phone and stood considering the matter. Then the scheme dropped into place, and she snapped her fingers.

Lindsey was watching the television set with both hands clamped over her eyes. "What are you doing?"

"I'm scared," the child said.

"Then why are you sitting here with the lights off?"

"I don't know."

"Well, come on, get your coat."

"My coat? Where are we going?"

"Across the street, to Tommy Doyle's."

"I don't like Tommy Doyle."

"That's tough. Tonight you're going to like Tommy Doyle, because tonight I'm going to *love* Paul."

"Do I have to?"

"Look, Lindsey, I thought we understood each other."

"Can you find out if Tommy is watching the same movie?"

"He will be. All you little masochists are watching the same movie."

"Oh, all right," the child finally said with obvious reluctance. "At least wait till the commercial."

Annie went to the coat closet and got Lindsey's parka and borrowed Mrs. Wallace's tweed coat. They waited for the next commercial, then Annie hustled the kid out the door, and they ran across the street.

In the tangle of a wisteria vine at the side of the Wallace's porch, the prowler stood, holding his knife. He watched the two girls cross the street and stand in front of the door of the house where the other girl was staying. He didn't risk going across yet, so he stood his ground, waiting to see what they did, feeling a throbbing between his legs and a painful pounding in his temples. The voice was getting louder. He had come close a few minutes ago, when the girl was stuck in the window, but the child had foiled it at the last second.

That was all right. He had all night. Opportunity would present itself again . . .

Annie rang the doorbell for the third time. At last the door opened a crack and Annie stepped back as the blade of a wicked-looking knife appeared in the door. "Who is it?" That was Laurie's voice, behind the knife.

"It's me, fool."

"Oh, Annie, thank God. I've been so jumpy." Laurie opened the door wide, lowering the blade, which glistened with orange pulp. Beside her stood Tommy Doyle.

"We're making a jack-o'-lantern," Tommy said to Lindsey.

"I want to watch TV," Lindsey said, zipping past the boy and into the television room.

Laurie looked at her friend's bizarre get-up, a brown tweed coat over a long blue robe. "Fancy," Laurie said.

"This has definitely not been my night," Annie replied, following her into the kitchen. "My clothes are in the wash, I spilled butter down the front of me, I got stuck in a window . . ."

"I'm glad you're here, because I've been thinking it over, and I have something I want you to do. I want you to call up Ben Tramer right now and tell him you were just fooling around."

"I can't."

"Yes, you can." Laurie gazed at her earnestly, her breast heaving with agitation.

"He went out drinking with Mike Godfrey,

so he won't be back until late. *You'll* have to call him tomorrow; that's all there is to it. Besides, I'm on my way over to Paul's."

"Huh? Wait a minute."

"Tell you what. If you'll watch Lindsey, I'll *consider* talking to Ben Tramer in the morning."

Laurie shook her head in a combination of admiration and exasperation. "You've got a deal."

They slapped palms.

"Hey, I thought Paul was grounded," Laurie remembered.

"He was. But his parents are going out. Listen, I'll call you in an hour or so." And before Laurie could say anything else, Annie rushed out the door.

She trotted across the street, the hem of her robe trailing after her like the gown of some regal bride. She went directly to the backyard and opened the door of the laundry room. This time she was smart, leaving a box of soap powder inside the door frame so that the door couldn't slam shut again. "Oh, Paul, I give you all," she sang, flinging open the door of the dryer. She grinned. The clothes weren't fluffy dry, exactly, but they were dry.

She stripped out of the robe and coat, pulled the red sweater on, jiggled into her skirt, and carried the discarded clothes back to the house. She found her purse and applied a light powder and blush to her cheeks, then traced an aggressive red line around her lips. "Ready for action," she told her image in the mirror.

The phone rang. "Hello?"

"Annie, it's me."

"Oh, hi, Dad."

"What are you doing?"

"Just watching TV with Lindsey."

"Good. Just be careful."

"Careful about watching TV?"

"No," the sheriff laughed, "just careful."

"Well, if you won't tell me, how can I be careful?"

"Keep the doors and windows locked, and call if you see or hear anything suspicious."

"The most suspicious thing I hear right now is you. But I understand. It's Sheriff Brackett's Standard Warning Number 305."

"No, it's a little more than that." His voice was deadly serious.

"Okay, Dad. I'll be sure to lock up."

"Good girl."

She hung up. "I'll be sure to lock up *after* leaving the house," she said aloud, feeling a little guilty about mocking her father. "Some good girl. If he could see me now." She picked up the house key from a dish on the foyer table and ran out of the house, locking the door.

She shivered as she stepped outside and walked around the side of the house to the garage. The sound of breaking branches startled her. "Lester, for God's sake stop creeping around in there."

She entered the garage, singing, "My Paul, I can no longer stall." She got into the car and snapped her fingers. "No keys, but please, my Paul, *da de da de da . . .*" She thought she'd left them in the ignition, but obviously they were in her purse. She ran back to the house, found them, and returned to the car.

Funny. She thought she'd left the car door closed when she left it a moment ago. "The old memory's going," she muttered. "Either that or the doors of the world have declared war on me." She wriggled into the driver's seat and inserted the key in the ignition.

Before she could turn it, he sat up in the back seat, massive and powerful, hideous in his rubber Halloween mask. She had time only to glimpse him in the mirror, the beat of her heart cascading into a runaway frenzy. She screamed, but the closed car doors and windows muffled the sound. A second later his immensely strong forearm was under her chin, crushing her windpipe. She beat and scratched at his arm, but it was futile. Her lungs tried desperately to suck air into her body. In one last effort to free herself, she pressed the horn on the rim of the steering wheel. It blared loudly in the night for a long moment. Then the knife plunged into her belly.

She could actually hear her mind contemplating the length and coldness of the long blade as it penetrated. But she didn't really feel any pain. The terror and resignation had made her impervious to it. She knew she was dead, and in her last moment she was aware of a blend of surprise and regret that the event could be so peaceful and undramatic. She wished she could have said a proper good-bye to her parents. She wished she'd understood her father's warning to be careful. She wondered if she'd be reborn and get a second chance to be careful. The light faded, and the last thing she heard was the car horn . . .

Across the street the children watched the *Creature from the Black Lagoon* swim out of its murky lair and glide toward the thrashing white legs of the pretty girl. Laurie was in the kitchen putting the finishing touches on the jack-o'-lantern.

Tommy got an idea for a prank. He sidled off the couch and slid behind a window curtain. Lindsey was so totally absorbed in the movie she didn't notice that her friend was no longer by her side. Suddenly, from the drapery behind her, a spooky voice called, *"Lindseeeyyyy, Lindseeeyyyyy."*

Lindsey jumped up in her seat. "Who's that? Tommy? Where are you?"

She jumped out of her seat and looked around the room, her little heart tripping with fright. She saw a bulge behind the curtain.

Behind the curtain Tommy happened to look out the window at that moment. He saw a huge dark figure with a white grotesque face carrying the limp body of a girl out of the Wallaces' garage. Tommy felt a surge of fear like none he'd ever known. *"The bogeyman!"* he cried, trying to charge out of the curtain but tangling himself in it. He felt something girdling his waist and pounding him. The air was filled with frightened wails.

Laurie rushed in and found Lindsey, Tommy, and the curtain tangled together, the children shrieking hysterically. She separated them and tried to hush them, but Tommy kept saying, "There he is, there he is! The bogeyman! I saw him again! He's over at Lindsey's house. The bogeyman, I'm telling you!"

Laurie held the boy in her arms. "Come on, Tommy, there's no bogeyman. Look."

"I won't look."

"Me either," said Lindsey, caught between the devil outside or the deep blue sea on the television screen. She chose the devil, but nothing was there. The street was empty. Her house looked the same as it always did. There was nothing, nobody.

"I saw him, I'm telling you. Carrying a dead body."

"Tommy, stop it! You're scaring Lindsey." Laurie shook the boy by the shoulders.

"He was big and tall and his face was like this . . ." He put his fingers in his lips and spread them apart.

"I said stop it! There is no bogeyman. There's nothing out there. If you don't quit it, I'm turning off the TV and sending you to bed."

That threat had the desired effect. Tommy

walked docilely back to the couch, followed by
Lindsey. They sat down as before, taking comfort
in the cinematic horror flickering before them.
"Nobody believes me," the boy complained under
his breath.

"I believe you, Tommy," said Lindsey, hug-
ging him.

The *Creature from the Black Lagoon* reached
out with a disgusting leathery claw and prepared
to grapple the ankle of the pretty swimmer . . .

13

On a dark cul-de-sac called Porter Lane, three
diminutive figures dressed in dark clothes
stealthily approached a large stone house. A big
picture window commanding a sweeping lawn revealed a family watching television: a father and
mother, a young girl, a baby boy, and an older
woman, presumably the grandmother.

The three dark shapes blended with the shadows like jaguars stalking prey. On a signal from
the one in the center the other two fanned
out, approaching the target window from the
flanks while the leader bellied toward the middle.

Now the three crouched directly underneath
the window, and the leader indicated it was time.
They donned their fright masks and rose up as
one with their soap bars. "Yaaarrrrghhh," they
roared, slamming their open palms on the window
while scrawling with the soap bars with their
free hands. The children went shrieking out of
the den. The older woman put her hand to her
heart and screamed silently. The mother gazed
stupidly, while the father, who was the only one
to grasp what was happening, stared in a combination of anger and amusement. He had probably
done the same when he was a kid.

Howling with laughter, Keith, Richie, and
Lonnie fled into the night, cutting across the frozen bed of the stream on the Samuels property

and slowing to a panting walk on Willow Circle.

"Did you see the look on the old lady's face?" Keith said.

"Yeah. I just hope she didn't have a heart attack," said Lonnie.

"Nah," Keith sneered, but for a moment he wondered.

"Now what?" Richie asked.

"*You* know what," said Keith.

"The Myers house, right?"

"Right. Look at Richie," Keith said to Lonnie. "He looks like we just asked him to drop his pants in Taft Square."

"Bullshit," the smallest of the three said.

"Then let's go. And you'll go in first."

"Fine," Richie said biting his lip.

They cut across the Henderson backyard and found themselves on the sidewalk two houses down from the Myers house. It stood, squat and dark and malevolent among its neighbors like some deformed creature. The gusty wind beat the branches of a huge untrimmed tree against the upper story.

"Okay, wiseass, lead the way," said Lonnie.

Richie stuck his chin out. "Sure. Watch." He strode arrogantly up to the front door, then faltered. He turned to his friends and gestured for them to follow. Lonnie and Keith stepped forward a few paces, bracing to run. "What are you afraid of?" Lonnie yelled.

"I'm not afraid."

"Bullshit. You're afraid of the bogeyman. You weren't afraid of him when you pushed Tommy Doyle around at school today."

"You pushed him too, you know, and I don't see you going into this house."

"We'll go in when you go in."

"All right, then stand right here behind me."

The two stragglers looked up. Faint silver

shadows flashed over the structure as clouds scudded before the moon. The wind gusted, quickening the tattoo of the branches on the clapboard upstairs.

All at once the bushes at the side of the house rattled and a human figure burst out. *"Get your asses away from there!"* it bellowed, waving its hands.

"Whoa!"

"Yikes!"

"Jesus!"

Moving like the wind, the three tumbled off the porch and hurtled down the street, not stopping until they were safely locked behind the doors of their homes.

Sam Loomis grinned. It was a dirty trick, but he had to get them out of there, both for their sakes and for his own. Now he went back to his blind watching and waiting, shivering in the cold night air.

He did not see the hand reach out for his shoulder, but at the first contact he whirled around in a fluid motion, the big gun materializing in his fist like a conjurer's hare.

"Hey, it's me, don't shoot!" Sheriff Brackett cried.

"Good God, Brackett, don't sneak up on me that way."

"Sorry, Loomis. It's second nature to me. Put that bazooka away."

"Yes, of course. I'm rather jumpy, as you can see."

"But you're all right."

"Sure. Has anything happened?"

Brackett shook his head. "Nothing going on. Just the usual, kids playing pranks, trick-or-treating, parking and necking, getting high. I have a feeling you're way off on this one."

"You have the wrong feeling," Loomis said firmly.

"You're not coming up with much to prove me wrong. Aside from one half-eaten dog . . ."

"Exactly what more do you need?"

"I don't know, but it's going to take a lot more than some sophisticated psychological interpretation to keep me up all night creeping around these bushes."

Loomis looked at him with a directness that made Brackett extremely uncomfortable. "I watched him for fifteen years, sitting in a room, staring *through* the walls, if you can understand that, staring through the walls and seeing *this night*. He's waited for it, planned for it, focused his life on it. He's inhumanly patient. Hour after hour, day after day, waiting for some silent, invisible alarm to trigger him—a voice to tell him the time has come, a gauge to tell him his blood has begun to boil. Death has arrived in your little town, Sheriff. You can ignore it, or you can help me stop it."

Brackett shook his head skeptically. "More fancy talk. You want to know what Haddonfield is? Families. Children. Nice homes, all lined up in white rows up and down these streets. Oak trees. Picket fences. An old school with a new annex, a lot of churches, all denominations. A five-and-dime, a hardware store, a beauty parlor, a coffee shop, some bars and gas stations. I'm describing a small midwestern town to you, Loomis, not a slaughterhouse."

"You could be describing both."

"I'll stay out with you tonight, Doctor, just on the chance that you're right. And if you *are* right, then damn you for letting him get out."

Loomis dropped his head. There was nothing he could say in reply.

His name was Bob Simms, and the girls all thought he was gorgeous. He was tall and lanky, a pitcher for the baseball team, a tight end for the football team. Possible valedictorian of the class, and at least one of its top three or four scholars. He could have any college he wanted, and any girl.

The girl he wanted on this particular night was Laurie and Annie's leggy blond friend, Linda.

Bob picked her up in his father's van, which had been customized as a recreational vehicle with a bunk bed in the back. Bob and Linda had made love back there many times, and though the car's heater worked they preferred to make love in a house now that cold weather had set in. So when Annie had gotten her babysitting gig with Lindsey Wallace, the two girls had worked out a plan. As soon as Lindsey went to sleep, Annie's Paul would come over and they'd make out upstairs in the Wallaces' bedroom, and Bob and Linda would do it downstairs on the convertible sofa. Good plan.

"You ready for a little trick or treat?" Bob asked her when he picked her up, yanking the tab off a can of Budweiser with a loud pop and a rush of foam.

"Sure," Linda laughed. They laughed, embraced, and guzzled, then drove over to the Wallace house.

As they pulled up in front of the Wallace home, Linda reviewed the plan. "Now, are you sure you've got it?"

"Sure. First I rip your clothes off . . ." He leaned across to the passenger's seat and buried his lips in Linda's soft neck while running a hand under her sweater.

She laughed and spilled beer over his head. "You idiot!"

"Then you rip my clothes off. Then we rip *Lindsey's* clothes off. I think I've got it."

"You've got something," she said, sliding

her hand up his muscular thigh. "Now *I've* got something."

"Jeez, Linda," Bob gasped with a rush of desire. "Let's pray for a sleeping Lindsey."

"Yes, but in case our prayers aren't answered, maybe we can drop some Valium in her chocolate milk."

"You're terrible."

"Totally," Linda said, pushing open the door.

Bob opened the door, got out, and helped Linda step down on the other side. They walked up the path to the big old house, and when they reached the front door Bob scooped Linda effortlessly into his arms and carried her the rest of the way. "Bob, put me down. Put me down! This is totally silly!" Linda protested, though her feeble kicks belied her protests. She reached out and turned the knob of the front door. The door swung open and the couple paused on the threshold. "Annie?"

The house was dark and still.

"Annie, we're here."

No answer.

They let their eyes adjust to the darkness, then stepped into the house. They cocked their ears and thought they heard a creak upstairs. They called Annie's name again. Again no answer. "I wonder if they're here at all," Bob said.

"Maybe they're upstairs already. Lindsey's asleep and Annie and Paul are up there already," Linda speculated.

Bob turned on a light. "I don't know. I don't want to be surprised in the middle of . . . well, in the middle. Let's look for a note."

"Let's don't," Linda said, turning the light off and sliding into his arms. He pressed his mouth to hers and her lips parted. Her tongue entwined his as her body melted against his powerful torso. He slid his hands over her back and clasped her buttocks, practically lifting her off the floor. "Now," she murmured, "shall we continue Plan A?"

"I guess," he said, leading her to the couch. "I just wish I could be sure about Annie and Paul." He went to the foot of the stairs and observed a light on under the door of the master bedroom. A faint creak came from there. He stood indecisively looking up.

Linda came up behind him and put her arms around him. "Bob, the only thing you have to worry about is getting up for the occasion."

"It's never been a problem before, and it shouldn't be now." He took her by the hand, and they lay down on the couch. Linda's body arched up at once as if the seat of the couch was molten metal. She urged her breasts and pelvis at her lover, and he took them avidly, pushing her sweater up to her neck and covering her breasts and belly with kisses. Her nipples contracted into hard nuggets under the flicking of his warm tongue, and his hand caressed her belly lovingly, his fingers gliding beneath the tops of her jeans and under the silky smoothness of her bikini panties. His fingers undid the top snap of the jeans and artfully slid the zipper down, his hand coming to rest on the silky crotch of her pants. She moaned and strained her body upward to receive his caresses.

In the shadow of the kitchen door he watched them. His breathing was heavy, but the noise of their excitement subdued the sound of his own.

After that incredible moment of thrill as he plunged the blade into the dark-haired girl's abdomen and slit her stomach open to the ribs, he had come down to a state of euphoric calm. For a while he had thought that the lust was permanently discharged and the voice quieted. That was how it had been then, with Judy.

But then he had been six years old, now it

was different. The sight of the couple on the couch had brought new stirring in his body, and the voice was whispering to him once more.

He knew this night was not over.

The phone rang, and he shrank back into the cover of darkness.

Bob and Linda sat up sharply, letting the phone ring three times in the hope that Annie would take it upstairs. The Wallaces would think it odd that someone other than their babysitter was picking up the phone. But when no one picked it up, Linda reached for the downstairs phone on the table beside the couch.

"Hullo," Linda said dreamily.

"Linda? Is that you?"

"Laurie? Hi!"

"Hi. What's happening?"

"Wouldn't you like to know," Linda giggled. "Hey, do you know where Annie is?"

"Yes, she's . . . Tommy, cut it out. Linda, just a sec."

In the background Linda heard a ghostly sound and screaming, then Laurie shouting, seeming to berate somebody. At length she got back on the phone.

"Sorry, Tommy was chasing Lindsey around with a pumpkin on his head."

"Lindsey's *there?*" Linda blurted.

"Uh-huh. See, Annie decided to go over to Paul's, so she left Lindsey here with me."

"Ah-so. That means we have the house to ourselves."

"Looks that way. But listen, would you please be sure to have Annie call me the second she gets back? I've got to get Lindsey back over there before her parents come home."

"Fine."

"Have a good time," Laurie said.

"We're planning to."

Linda hung up and grabbed Bob by the hand.

"Well, old boy, it looks as if we've got the house all to ourselves, including the bed upstairs."

Bob laughed. "Well now, to use your favorite phrase, that sounds totally fantastic. Shall we go?"

He offered his arm and she grasped it. "Thank you, kind sir." He led the way up the stairs, hesitating before the door to the master bedroom because the door was closed and a light streamed under it and into the hallway, a flickering orange light. Then he shrugged and opened the door. They laughed.

On the night table a jack-o'-lantern flickered.

"Well, Mr. Jack-o'-lantern, you're going to see some things tonight," Linda said, patting it on its poll. "How about this for starters?" Facing the pumpkin's grotesque grin, she did a sensuous strip tease, wriggling out of her sweater and jiggling her breasts, cupping them with her hands in mute offering to the pumpkin, then bumping and grinding out of her jeans until she was prancing before the jack-o'-lantern in bikini panties.

Bob laughed, reaching out and grabbing her wrist. "I'm jealous."

"Of a pumpkin?"

"Well, if you're into squashes so much, try this zucchini," he said, putting her hand on the rocklike bulge under his jeans.

"*Mmm*, I have a sudden hunger for zucchini," she whispered, helping him unbuckle his belt and unbutton his jeans.

His knees began to weaken and he leaned on her shoulders for support. Then, when he could stand it no longer, he pulled her to her feet and toward the bed.

Bob grinned and sat astride her, kneading her breasts until the nipples were like stones. Her hips writhed under him, her pelvis thrusting involuntarily in circular motions.

He needed no coaxing. Kneeling between her

quivering thighs, he slid into her up to the hilt, and her moan of pleasure filled the room with its primitive timbre. He wrapped his arms tightly around her slim, firm waist and she covered his broad back with sharp-nailed fingers. He pumped rhythmically into her, her hips stropping him to an awesome height of need and pleasure. "Oh, Bob, I think . . . I think it's happening," she whimpered.

"Me too."

And that's when the phone rang.

Bob stopped in mid-stroke, gripped with uncertainty.

"Shit! Not again!"

"Forget about it," Linda said. "We have more important things to do." The phone sounded again.

"What if it's Annie?"

"She'll call us again."

"And what if it's the Wallaces?"

"If it's the Wallaces and we answer, we'll get Annie into trouble."

"Yeah, but what if . . . ?"

"What if it's your mommy?" Linda taunted.

Bob laughed. "I'll just tell her I'm really into something right now that I can't get out of. There, it's stopped. I'll take it off the hook."

He reached across her body to the night table, where the jack-o'-lantern guarded the telephone, and took the phone off its cradle. Then he turned his attention back to her. "Now, where were we?"

"Old Mr. Zucchini's getting soft enough to mash," she said, stroking him with artful grinds of the pelvis. "There, that's better."

"Oh, yes, that's better. That's much better."

He stood in the hall watching them resume their coupling, and the desire returned. His fingers caressed the handle of his knife in rhythm to the powerful strokes of the man's buttocks against the widespread girl's body. The voice spoke loudly to him, urging him to act, but he held himself back, anxious to see the climax of their performance.

He was soon rewarded. "Oh Bob, I think it's going to happen now . . . now . . . now!"

"Yes, *yes*, YES!" Bob cried, nailing her to the bed with his lanky, powerful body.

Their voices mingled moans and pants and endearments as they thrashed the last lust out of one another's flesh. Then they lay still for a minute or two, the boy's back a tempting target for the blade of the man who stood outside their door, breathing deeply but silently. No, not yet.

At length Bob rolled off Linda and groped around the floor for his shirt. He found it and produced a pack of cigarettes and lit two, giving her one. They lay on their backs, blowing thin streams of smoke into the air.

"Fantastic," Linda sighed. "Totally fantastic."

"Yeah."

"Want a beer?"

"Yeah."

"Is that all you have to say?"

"Yeah."

"Go get me a beer."

"I thought you were gonna get one for me," Bob said.

"*Yeah?*"

"Oh well." Reluctantly, Bob climbed out of bed and stepped into his jeans. Then he groped around the floor for his glasses and found them at last, donning them.

Linda looked at him. "Do you really need those?"

"I only wear them when I'm looking for beer," he replied with a grin. "I'll be right back." He leaned over the bed and kissed her. "Don't get dressed."

Silently, the visitor withdrew from his observation place outside the door and drifted soundlessly down the stairs, taking his place in the large utility closet in the kitchen. He waited and listened, knife poised. In due time, through the slightly open door, he saw the boy come into the kitchen. He had on jeans but no shirt or shoes and socks, and he wore horn-rimmed glasses. The boy's body was sleek, hairless, and muscular.

Bob went directly to the refrigerator in the dark and opened the door, sending a stream of light across the kitchen floor. He took two beers out, closed the door, and opened a cupboard. "Peanuts, peanuts, peanuts . . . ah, here they are. And potato chips are . . . here."

He gathered the food in his arms and turned to leave, but didn't see the legs of a stool half under a counter, and he tripped, dropping everything. Muttering, he stooped and picked it up. Then he heard the creak of a door behind him.

Arms loaded, he freed a hand and opened the kitchen door. "Annie? Paul?" he called. "No jokes, huh? I'm in the midst of something very important." No answer. He closed the door and locked it. Then he heard the creak again and realized it was coming from the utility closet. He put the beer and food down on the counter and stealthily approached the door. Then he flung it open. "Okay, Linda, come on out. Come on, I know it's . . ."

The thing lunged out like a leaping tiger, its left hand gripping Bob's neck in a death-clutch. Bob fell back, grabbing at his throat, then swung at the head of his tormentor. The man took the blow full on the face, but it didn't faze him. He slammed Bob up against the wooden pantry door and lifted him clear off the tile floor by the throat. Gurgling noises came from his windpipe as he clawed at the rubber mask on his assailant's face. If Bob was going to escape he'd have to make his best shot now, because the oxygen supply was rapidly dwindling and he knew he had but a few seconds. He cupped his hands over his head and brought them down with full force on the man's head. It shook him but failed to weaken his grip on Bob's throat. Out of the corner of his eye Bob saw the blade in the man's free hand, and he brought his knees up in a helpless gesture of self-protection. He actually heard the *whap* of the knife as the killer drove it into his gut with stupendous force. Then the blackness came over him.

The killer held himself against the twitching body, then stepped away. The body went limp but the knife had penetrated all the way into the pantry door, and Bob hung impaled on it, feet dangling about six inches from the floor. His eyes were wide with horror. His tongue drooped stupidly out of the corner of his lips.

Linda dragged impatiently on her cigarette, then ground it out in the ashtray on the night table, just under the grimacing mouth of the jack-o'-lantern. "Well, Jack, where is he? I sent him down ten minutes ago for one lousy beer. Is he manufacturing it or what? If he were half the man he looks like, he'd have made the round trip in record time and would be back in bed by now. Isn't that right, Jack?" The pumpkin's flame answered her with mute flickering. Linda tapped another cigarette out of the pack and hung it on her lower lip. Then she grinned with inspiration. "Hey, baby, light my fire," she said to the jack-o'-lantern, thrusting the cigarette through the pumpkin's nose and lighting it on its candle. "Thanks. You may look like a punk, but deep down inside, you're a real gentleman. Not like some people."

She heard the steps creaking and composed herself under the covers. The steps were heavy, like an old man's or someone laboring under a big load. "Thank God," Linda sighed. "Where's my beer?"

The door opened and she laughed, shaking her head. He wore a sheet over his head with eyes cut out, and over the eyes he wore Bob's heavy glasses. He stood inside the door, staring at her, breathing in long sighing wheezes that blew the sheet away from his mouth with each exhalation. "Cute, Bob. Real cute. Come here, you fool."

He came no closer.

"I'll bet I can get your ghost," she said, sliding the sheet teasingly off her chest.

Linda laughed at her own joke, but when the ghost remained planted in the doorway, she frowned and brusquely pulled the sheets back up around her throat. "All right, all right. So where's the beer?"

No response.

"Well, answer me! Okay, don't answer me. Boy, are you weird." Still no response. The ghost stood fixed to his spot like a tree. "Bob, enough's enough, you're making me nervous." No response. "Oh, shit. Okay for you." She got out of bed. Completely nude, she walked to the pile of clothes at the foot of the bed. In the soft glow of the candle she looked incredibly beautiful. She did not walk so much as glide. She knew what effect she had on men, and if this didn't do the trick, Bob must be made of brick. She pulled her panties out of the pile and dangled them in front of the ghost's glasses, stroking them with her other hand. "Last chance, pal, before I hide the jewels." She paused, waiting for a reply. Then she shrugged. "Okay." She stepped into her panties and turned away.

"Well, I'm going to call Laurie. I want to know where Annie and Paul are. *This* isn't going anywhere." She picked up the phone and pivoted, turning her back on the ghost. She dialed the Doyles' number.

The ghost began to advance. Linda could see him coming out of the corner of her eye. While she waited for Laurie to pick up the phone, she said, "Well, I finally got you to make your move. I knew it. As soon as I hide my ass, you want to pull my pants down. You men are all ali——*arrgggghh...*"

He clamped one hand over her mouth and with the other wrapped the phone cord around her throat. She reacted with the ferocity of a victim in full panic, clawing at his knuckles with sharp nails and tearing strips of flesh off the back of his hands. He gripped her more tightly despite the searing pain. On the other end of the phone line he could hear someone saying, "Hello? Hello?"

He gripped the wire tighter. The girl danced madly in his clutches, biting, kicking, wriggling, scratching, pounding, pulling, striking. She fought harder than any of them, fought with amazing pluck, but it was all for nought. All for nought. Her movements began to slow down and become more jerky and frenetic. Her face was turning blue, and her tongue flopped around her lips as if it had no organic connection with the rest of her body. Her eyes bulged like a frog's, the red blood vessels in the whites bursting with the overload.

With one last frantic effort she aimed ten fingernails at his eyes, but he buried his face in the back of her neck so that she had no good target. Her nails tangled in the bedsheet. When her hands went limp at last, they dragged the sheet with them, revealing her assassin.

He wore a grotesque mask.

"Hello? Hello?" Laurie tapped her fingernails impatiently on the phone. "All right, Annie! I've heard your famous chewing, now I get your famous squeals?"

The gurgles and sputters continued. "Annie? Annie, are you all right?" Now she heard a heavy, throaty breathing. "Annie, are you fooling around again? Annie, I'll kill you if this is a joke. Oh, God, I can't wait for this day to end," she said, slamming the phone down.

She went to the window and looked across the street. Bob's van was still parked there, but except for an orange glow from an upstairs window, all the lights in the Wallace house were out. Laurie decided to phone there one more time; if nobody answered, she'd have to run across the street.

She dialed the Wallace number and waited. The phone rang four, five, six, seven times. With each ring, Laurie prayed harder that the joke would be over, that Linda or Bob or Annie or Paul would pick it up and, with their inimitable laughter, tell her it was all a big put-on. Eight rings, nine, ten.

Eleven, twelve, thirteen.

Fourteen, fifteen, sixteen . . .

14

Laurie put the phone down heavily and stood beside it, pondering her options. It was not so much that she didn't know what she must do; it was that she didn't want to do what she knew she must.

She tiptoed upstairs. Tommy and Lindsey were sprawled on Tommy's bed like a couple of rag dolls dropped from ten feet, hands and feet dangling over the sides and an assortment of dolls, game pieces, cars, trucks, fire engines, and Erector set components covered the bed and floor as if all had been packed into the muzzle of a mortar and fired indiscriminately into the room. Tommy was in his pajamas, but Lindsey, who had not been expected to stay so late, was still in her clothes.

Laurie felt safe in leaving them; she knew from countless babysitting assignments with them that their deepest slumber was immediately after falling asleep. They would not wake up and, not finding her in the house, push the panic button.

She went back downstairs and opened her purse. She had a ring with four or five keys belonging to the people she regularly sat for, and she selected the one to the Wallace house. She opened the front door of the Doyle house, stepped outside, and looking ruefully across the street, closed it behind her. She crossed the street and stood before the Wallace house, studying its hulking vastness for a sign of life. Except for the mellow flicker of a candle upstairs, there was none. She glanced in Bob's van, but nobody was in it either.

Her feet felt as if they'd been fitted with leaden shoes as she walked the last few yards and mounted the steps to the verandah encircling the house. She tested the knob of the front door. There was no need for her key. The door swung open.

She peered inside, listening. She thought she heard a floorboard groan, but perhaps not. She stepped inside and stood in the arched entrance to the living room. "Annie? Bob? Linda?"

The total silence that greeted her sent a shudder down her spine. She reached for the wall switch and flipped it.

The room remained dark. Cursing, she retreated to the entry hall and tried the switch to the big chandelier there.

No response.

"You guys have *really* been blowing some fuses," she said with a nervous laugh.

She stayed in the hall a moment, letting her eyes adjust to the darkness. Then she ventured into the living room. It was devoid of life, but an examination of the rumpled pillows on the couch indicated that some heavy petting had gone on. They were probably upstairs.

All of them? she wondered. "Oh Lord, just what I need—walking in on an orgy," she said aloud.

She jumped when she heard something heavy, like furniture, being moved upstairs, followed by a crash. She rushed to the foot of the stairs and stared up. The bedroom door was closed, but an eerie orange light radiated from under it.

She managed a smile, shaking her head. "All right, meatheads. The joke is over." She took one tentative step up the stairs and paused to listen. "Come on, Annie, enough."

A new sound greeted her, the sound of something being dragged across the floor. The sound stopped abruptly, followed by a closet door shutting in the upstairs bedroom.

Laurie took three more steps. "This has definitely stopped being funny, guys. Now cut it out!"

Now a scraping sound.

Her heart began to thunder and she thought of fleeing, but she knew what kind of laughing-stock she'd be at school if she did, when Annie and Paul and Linda and Bob told everybody how they'd scared Laurie Strode out of her shoes on Halloween.

"You'll be sorry!" she shouted as she made her way up the stairs with determination.

Sam Loomis was cold, and getting colder.

Had he known he'd be staked out in a hedge in the middle of a cold October night, he'd have dressed for the occasion. But he had worn his trench coat over a summer business suit, and he was cold.

Aside from the three kids he'd chased off, there'd been no activity at the Myers house, and as the evening wore into night Loomis began to wonder why he had expected that there would be. Yes, the fellow had returned to the scene of the crime in the best tradition of criminals, but that was much earlier. To what end would he hang around the house? Wouldn't he seek elsewhere for victims?

Because he was cold, and because he'd begun to realize he was barking up the wrong tree, Loomis started to pace. He paced up the block and down, glancing over his shoulder often so as not to take his attention totally off the Myers house. He paced in an ever-lengthening pattern, and the more he did, the more certain he became that his quarry was near. His conclusion was based on reason and emotion. Intellectually, he reasoned that with the strange affection of a hunter for his prey, his maniac had indeed come home today, and he'd seek victims in the immediate neighborhood.

But it wasn't just intellectual deduction; it was a feeling, a hunch. Loomis's spine quivered like a divining rod near water. Evil was afoot, and it was nearby. If only he could get some definite sign ...

Loomis's pacing swept him farther and farther away from the Myers house, and soon he was turning his back on it with impunity, for he was now convinced his maniac was not there. Back and forth like a pendulum Loomis swung, attuning himself to the vibrations of evil in the air and trying to get a fix on them like a pilot seeking radio guidance on a stormy night.

He debated with himself as to whether he should continue going straight up and down the block, or turn corners and form a kind of search grid with his pacing. At a certain corner he felt strongly drawn and decided to let the force carry him even if he lost sight of the Myers house entirely. It was as if he were the planchette on a ouija board and someone had asked him, *Is a murderer near at hand?* The force of the vibrations was sending him . . . where? Down this oak-lined street and toward that car. Why that car?

But it was not a car, it was a station wagon. A station wagon! Could it be the one? His pace quickened. It was hard to tell the color of the vehicle because of the yellow arc-light of the street lamps overhead, but it seemed to be that livid purplish brown of the state hospital's station wagon. One glance at the side of the vehicle would

tell him. He strained his eyes seeking the emblem
on the door, his legs churning at a pace they
hadn't done for a decade. And inside his head, the
vibrations of evil grew immeasurably stronger
with each yard he covered . . .

She stood on the landing, paralyzed with uncertainty. At the foot of the stairs she'd been certain this was a big put-on by her friends. But
with each step she mounted, her doubts had
mounted too. If this were a practical joke, it
was, well, too good, too professional. Where were
the whispering and the giggling, the shushing
and the tittering? There was too much silence.
Entirely too much silence.

She peered at the crack under the door, a
mellow orange line that shimmered seductively
like a neon sign advertising some forbidden de-
light. She clenched her teeth. If this was a setup,
they were doing a terrific job—special effects and
everything! How could she not go in?

She stepped forward two paces and encircled the doorknob with her hand. The muscles of
her legs were tensed like those of a runner at the
start of a race, prepared to spring back and down
the stairs at the first sign of trouble.

She pushed the door open a crack. She could
see a pair of feet on the bed, but whose she
couldn't yet identify. Just out of the range of
her vision, a candle or jack-o'-lantern cast an
orange light on the legs.

Laurie opened the door two inches farther
and stuck her head into the bedroom. She took
in more and more of the figure on the bed. The
feet, the knees, the thighs, the pubic hair, the
pelvis, the . . .

. . . the belly slit from waist to throat . . .

. . . the intestines spilled out on the bed lin-
ens . . .

... the gash across the throat, splashed with crimson blood ...

... the white, bloodless face of Annie, a silent scream on her mouth, the lucid horror of doom in her wide eyes ...

And behind her head, a tombstone.

The tombstone said:

Our Beloved Daughter
Judith Margaret Myers

There were dates, but Laurie did not read them because things happened too fast from that moment on.

She heard her own scream and realized in an instant that whatever it was that had slaughtered her best friend must be here, near, waiting for her. It was then that she caught sight of Bob, suspended by the throat from a rope tied around a ceiling fixture. His tongue, purple and bloated, dangled idiotically from swollen lips, and bloody gore spilled from a fist-sized hole in his abdomen.

Laurie's legs seemed to melt beneath her, and her will to flee flowed out of them as if released by a spigot. The time it took her to turn seemed like a week, but as she did pivot a closet on her right opened, revealing Linda, propped up in a chair, nude. From the neck down, unlike Annie and Bob, her body was unmarred. But her neck and face were livid with broken blood vessels as if some stupendous force had squeezed all her blood up into her head until the pressure had burst every capillary in her skin. Her red eyes all but bulged out of her head on their stalks and her tongue slavered over her lower lip like a mongoloid's.

If Laurie was screaming now, the pounding fear in her brain made it impossible for her to hear it. For someone whose experience of horror had been limited up to that moment to the sight of small animals run over on the highway, the load on her circuits was tantamount to sending a million volts through a wire designed to carry a hundred. What prevented her from passing out at that instant she did not know, but a voice inside her brain demanded that she take measures to survive, and she concentrated on it despite every instinct to submit to blind panic.

At the same moment that she came to this conclusion she saw the shadow, dark and dreadful, looming up in the flicker of the jack-o'-lantern. She knew it was the man who'd been dogging her steps that day, and she knew that he expected her to drop backward so that he could catch her off balance. So she did something illogical, and it saved her life.

She ducked.

She dropped to her haunches as he lunged for her. His hand swiped at her neck as he tripped over her shoulder, grabbing and tearing the arm of her blouse, but he got no more of her than that. But now she had a bigger problem, for he'd sprawled on the landing, blocking her way down the stairs. He grunted and rose to his feet slowly, almost casually; he had her cornered, and it was just a matter of closing the gap. He reached into his belt and drew out a huge knife clotted with blood. Laurie backed away, wondering if she could lure her attacker away from the stairs, but as he advanced on her, he kept his body between her and the landing.

Like a computer, her brain assessed the possibilities. She could retreat into the bedroom and try to bar the door. Too chancy. She could flee into another room. That was no safer.

Or she could dive over the stairway railing and take her chances with the drop.

That's what it had to be. She glanced over the rail and estimated it to be eight or ten feet to the first floor. She braced for the leap just as he was bracing for his. She sprang, placing her hand on the rail as if it were a gymnastic horse, and boosted her legs over it. For a second she clutched the railing to cushion the drop. She felt his hand close around hers as she released her grip on the railing. His grip was tremendously strong, but he was in an awkward position. Trying desperately to hold her with his left hand, he swiped at her with the knife in his right, but it grazed her arm and he released her. She tried to make her feet land squarely on the steps below, but her right foot caught one step poorly and a sharp pain shot up her ankle. Her right arm burned where the tip of his knife had caught her. As she clutched it she felt the wetness of blood.

But she was alive, and now she had to get out of here. She could see him doubled over the railing, but he recovered quickly and made for the landing. Laurie climbed to her feet. The pain in her ankle was excruciating, but she managed to hobble toward the kitchen. She heard him stumping down the stairs.

As she reached the security of the kitchen, she could see him turning the bend off the stairway, the steel of his knife blade glinting with reflected light from the street lamps. She flung the kitchen door shut and grabbed a steel chair from the dinette table. She propped it under the doorknob a scant second before she felt the thud of his shoulder against the door and heard his muffled grunt of frustration.

She limped to the outside door and turned the knob. It was locked or jammed, probably intentionally, probably by the same hand that had knocked out the lights. She groped for the button that she knew unlocks some types of storm door, but she couldn't find it.

All of a sudden the other door exploded as his fist penetrated it, sending wooden shrapnel

spraying across the room. The door boards
groaned and splayed inward as his arm sank
through them to the shoulder. Laurie watched
with round-eyed fascination before returning to
her task of getting out. She shook the knob in
desperation, but did little more than rattle the
glass. Behind her she could hear him widening
the hole in the door with a second splintering
punch.

Well, she told herself, struggling to keep her
wits, if he can smash his door, I can smash mine.
She looked around for a blunt instrument or even
a towel to cushion her hand from the glass shards,
but finding none and hearing the chair propping
up the other door sliding to the floor, she balled
her fist and struck the pane nearest the knob. It
shattered and she felt a dozen glass claws rup-
turing the flesh of her knuckles, but if there was
pain it was overridden by driving fear and desperation. She groped for a lock and found a little
butterfly bolt under the knob. She twisted it and
turned the inside knob with her other hand, shoving the frame with her shoulder. The door gave
and she fell outside just as she heard him kicking
the chair out of his way and lumbering across
the kitchen floor.

Still guided by a semblance of reason, she
shut the door behind her and twisted the lock to
give herself another few seconds of time. As she
picked herself up and limped toward the house
next door, she heard his grunted frustration upon
finding the second door locked. He tried to rattle
the door off its frame, and she could hear every
pane of glass vibrating.

She leaned against the doorbell of the Mar-
tinson home, which she knew to be occupied by
an aged and not particularly friendly couple. It
seemed to take an eternity for them to respond,
but a light did go on. She pounded on the door

shrieking, "Please, help me! Call the police! Please!"

She saw a hand part a shade and an eye peer out at her. "Please, call the police!" she shouted at the face. The window lifted an inch.

"No more trick or treat! It's late. Go away! We have no more candy!"

"Oh, God!" Laurie groaned as the light went out. At that moment she heard a pane of glass smash and her pursuer's hand thumping on the outside of the side door looking for the lock.

Dragging her bad ankle, she made her way across the street. She looked over her shoulder and saw the side door burst open and the black shape stagger out into the driveway. He looked around, then spotted her. She was almost at Doyles' front door.

The key. Where was the key?

She had clutched a ring of keys in her hand when she entered the Wallace home. Her jeans had been too tight to stuff a keyring into her pocket, so she had carried them into the house. And somewhere in the melee she had dropped them.

He was coming after her in steady, unhurried steps, knife bared as if daring the world to stop him. Anyone looking out at the scene would see a Halloween mime presented by a couple of clever youngsters. Why, those shrieks of hers were so bloodcurdling, they might be the real thing. And look how cunningly he'd painted that knife blade to look like blood!

Laurie pounded the door with the flat palm of her hand. "Tommy! Tommy, open the door! I'm locked out!" She thumped with her closed fist. "Tommy, wake up, it's me, Laurie!"

She looked around her and found a geranium planter beside the door mat. She picked it up, stepped back, and threw it at the bedroom win-

dow where Tommy and Lindsey were sleeping.
Please, God ...

Smash!

"Tommy, wake up, it's me, Laurie!"

She stood helplessly waiting for that welcome
face to appear in the window. She continued
shouting. The shape was halfway across the street
now, the features of his face resolving under the
street light. Either it was a rubber mask or a
real face too hideous to imagine. *"Tommy!"*

A sleepy face peered out of the broken glass.
"Laurie?"

"Tommy, hurry down here and open the door.
Hurry!"

The face disappeared and Laurie prayed
the kid didn't think he was dreaming and go back
to bed. The murderer was on the lawn now and
loping toward her, knife poised. Laurie's mind
flashed on the sight of Annie with her belly
ripped open and her guts hanging out on the
bed. "Tommy, hurry!"

The blessed sound of a bolt being thrown
open. She twisted the doorknob and shoved her
way inside, knocking Tommy down. She slammed
the door and twisted the lock and drove home a
second bolt as Tommy picked himself up and
rubbed his eyes.

"Tommy, I want you to go back upstairs ..."

"What is it, Laurie?"

"Be quiet! Get Lindsey and get back into the
bedroom and lock the door."

"I'm scared ..."

"Do what I say! Now!"

He backed away toward the stairs. "Laurie?"

"What?"

"It's the bogeyman, isn't it?"

"Hurry!"

Tommy burst into hysterical sobs as he
scampered up the stairs. The bedroom door
slammed and clicked as Tommy locked it. She

could hear Tommy and Lindsey making each other crazy with fear, but there was no time to spare to calm them down. She dashed for the phone and picked it up, waiting for a dial tone, finger poised over the dial. No dial tone. The phone was dead. She slammed it down and stood paralyzed, trying to determine her next move.

A breeze rippled through the air, rustling through her hair. It was coming from the kitchen. She took one step toward the kitchen, then stopped and backed away. If the door was already open, it was too late. He was already in the house.

Now it overwhelmed her. The reality of evil, the horror of reality, penetrated to a brain that since birth had been programmed to perceive horror and evil as something that could be contained within the perimeter of a nineteen-inch television tube. The shock was so violent she thought she would go mad. She buried her face and let out a mournful wail followed by choking sobs. "Please, please stop," she whimpered, sinking to her knees before the living room couch. "Please?"

She became aware of another sound in the room.

Someone was breathing heavily. And advancing on her.

"Please . . . ?"

Sam Loomis ran up the street, head tilted like a bloodhound trying to pick up a scent, except this wasn't a smell he was seeking but a feeling, a vibration. "You're getting hot; no, you're getting cold; no, you're getting hot again, hotter; no, colder," a voice seemed to say to him. His eyes searched house after house hoping to detect something out of kilter, but he was greeted with the disappointing sight of prim house after prim house nestled beneath sheltering trees on pleasantly manicured lawns. If only this were nineteenth-century Transylvania, he said blackly to himself, I'd know where to search, but this is the last quarter of the twentieth century in a lovely suburban town in the Midwest in modern America. Surely any manifestation of evil would shine like a beacon!

"Goddamn your soul, show yourself!" he cried at the night sky.

A pair of headlights pinned him as a police car swerved onto the street. The car pulled to an abrupt halt next to him. "Where the hell were you?" Brackett shouted from his window. Loomis could see his face flushed with rage. "I went back to the Myers house . . ."

Loomis impatiently waved him quiet. "I found the hospital station wagon. He's here!"

"Where's the car?"

"Three blocks down. Look, you go up this street and back down the next one. I'll go this way and criss-cross you. Honk your horn if you see anything. Fire your gun if it's serious. I'll fire mine."

"And if I see him?"

"Fire your gun . . . at his heart."

15

With death near at hand, a host of crazy thoughts tumbled through Laurie's brain. It was not exactly as they said, your life passing before your eyes. It was more like random snapshots of herself pulled from an unsorted collection: a trip to a Michigan lake with her father, when their canoe was blown ashore by a violent sudden squall; a two-layer cake baked with her mother, and the discovery they'd made only enough icing for one layer; a baby raccoon she'd kept for a pet until it tore up the den in a fit of rage.

She wondered what it would have been like to go to bed with a man; she wondered who would come to her funeral; she wondered what grades your teachers gave you if you died mid-term; she wondered what they'd dress her in for the funeral, and whether her face would be mutilated when they opened the coffin; she wondered what would have happened if she'd kept her date with Ben Tramer.

She wondered what it was like to die, and to be dead.

She sat at the foot of the couch almost serenely, like a condemned person awaiting execution. Beside her lay Mrs. Doyle's knitting kit. The needles ...

The needles!

Her bloodstained hand enclosed one of the

long needles at the precise moment his forearm encircled her neck. His arm might have been carved out of mahogany, it was so solid and muscular, and for the instant before she acted it clamped off her windpipe as effectively as a steel vise. She smelled the vile reek of blood on his arm and the stench of his breath. She knew that if she hesitated even two seconds it would all be over, for even if he did not strangle her to death, the blade in his other hand might even now be describing the arc that would terminate in her belly.

Measuring her next move carefully, knowing it might be her last if she were wrong, she thrust the eight-inch needle over her shoulder in the vicinity of his face. She felt it sink deeply into flesh.

She heard a grunt, and his forearm relaxed long enough for her to slide out from under it. She ran for the stairs, looking behind her for just a heartbeat. He was staggering back from the couch, clawing at a needle buried in his neck. She ascended the staircase three steps at a time despite the agonizing pain in her swollen ankle.

She pounded on the locked bedroom door. "It's me, Tommy, Lindsey. It's me. Open the door, hurry."

Tommy opened the door and peeked out. She rushed into the room, knocking the kid on his behind for the second time. She kicked the door shut and locked it. The children's faces were stained with tears, and their eyes rolled involuntarily. They were perilously close to passing out from shock. She embraced them, shushing them. "It's all right, kids. Shhh, it's all . . ."

She cocked her head. She could hear movement downstairs. Furniture being shoved around, heavy footsteps staggering toward the stairs.

"Now," she said, fighting desperately to contain the fear savaging her chest, "I want you to change your clothes, Tommy. We're going to take a walk outside."

"It was the bogeyman, wasn't it?" the boy said, his little body trembling like a trapped animal's.

"No," said Laurie, listening. There was a heavy thud at the foot of the stairs, then silence. She brightened. If that noise was what she hoped it was, the threat was over. "No, it wasn't."

"I'm so scared," whimpered Lindsey.

"There's nothing to be scared of now," she reassured the little girl. Again she listened. It was quiet.

"Are you sure?" Tommy pleaded.

"Yes."

"How do you know?"

"Because I killed him."

"But you can't kill the bogeyman."

"I can, and I did. He's lying at the foot of the..."

Her sentence was shattered along with her peace of mind by a tremendous blow on the door. It held, but the panel closest to the knob arched inward, showering the floor with paint chips. The next blow would shatter it.

Though the fight had all but drained out of her, Laurie moved instinctively to save the children, hustling them into the bathroom. They bawled like cattle in a slaughterhouse as she closed the door on them, shouting "Lock it! Lock the door!" She waited ten lifetimes for the click, and wondered what good it did to lock doors when this beast was able to shatter them like rice-paper screens. Already his fist had broken through the weakened panel and was groping for the lock. She would have liked to strike that vulnerable hand with a heavy weapon, but she couldn't leave her post until the kids locked their door. "Tommy . . . !"

The bolt clicked on the bathroom door just as the bolt on the bedroom door gave. Laurie backed away, looking around the room for a weapon or someplace to hide, but nothing better than a louvred walk-in clothes closet presented itself. She dashed for it, parting the double doors and slamming them closed behind her.

She noticed a tie rack just inside the door, and she now grabbed a tie and wrapped it around the little porcelain doorknobs so as to hold the double doors closed. What good this would do she didn't know, and she laughed grimly to think that anyone who could punch through half-inch plywood would be fazed by a door of thin pine slats held closed by a necktie. But perhaps it would buy her three seconds to think, to prepare, to defend herself.

Or maybe it would merely buy her three more to live.

She heard the bedroom door burst open and his stumping footsteps enter the room. He growled as he breathed, and again the reek of her friends' blood freshly spilled on his hands permeated the room.

She moved farther back into the closet and sent some empty hangers jingling to the floor. *Nice going, Laurie,* she said to herself. *Why didn't you just shout, "I'm in here, Mr. Murderer!"*

He shuffled toward the closet and rattled it with tornadolike force. Laurie retreated to a corner of the closet and slumped to the floor. *So this is where you die,* she declared inwardly.

A second later the fist came through the louvres with the ease of a hammer smashing a balsa toy. The blood-clotted hand swept the closet, fingers seeking a piece, any piece, of Laurie's body, but finding only clothes and hangers. These fell on her, and with them fell on her exhausted mind the only, the last, thing to do before succumbing to the assassin's crazed assault.

She picked up a wire hanger.

She began to untwist the handle, which consisted of the two ends of the heavy-gauge wire wrapped around themselves. As the killer's hands played up and down the louvre slats she at last managed to separate the two ends of the wire and unbend the hanger. She grasped it tightly halfway up and held it ready.

The door hung on a splinter. The next strike would destroy it. Sure enough, it belled in, buckled, and exploded in a million fragments, and Laurie seemed to see them all in sharply focused slow motion, like the fragments of a life blasted beyond recognition—a father, a mother, a home, a school, a friend, a past, a future, a present . . .

The snarling thing was inside the closet with her, lashing out at the limp clothing and sweeping it aside or tossing it to the floor. The ferocity of it was wonderful to see, and some detached, dispassionate part of her watched the performance with admiration, as if it were a circus ring and she safely stood outside.

Then she was no longer a spectator. She was now the prize at the bottom of the bin. Though dark as a coal mine, she could see that he had turned away from the far corner of the closet and now faced her, his eyes as keenly focused in the darkness as hers were. They confronted one another silently except for the hiss of their breath. There followed a moment when Laurie fantasized that he would not make his lunge, that he would tear off his mask and laugh and say it was all a Halloween prank and the bodies across the street were just cleverly made-up store dummies and you could get up now and go home and we'll see you next Halloween.

Or maybe he had decided he'd had enough slaughter for one night and would turn away and deliver himself into the hands of the police. Or maybe he'd succumb at this very last instant to

the wound in the neck she'd inflicted in his neck
with Mrs. Doyle's needle.

*Sure, Laurie, sure. Still dreaming right up
to the last, aren't you?*

Slowly, deliberately, he drew the knife out of
his belt and knelt before her, gauging the precise
spot where he would plunge the blade in. She wondered what part of her he would consider prime.
He seemed to be studying her the way a butcher studies the carcass of a steer.

She clutched the wire hanger with both
hands and concentrated on the one vulnerable
area she thought she could damage. She felt his
hot stinking breath on her face and knew he
would never be closer while she lived. With a
prayer to God she thrust the hanger into the
black hole in the mask where a glint of eyeball
reflected what scant light there was in the room.
For a second there was resistance, as if the wire
had struck his cheekbone or nose or eyebrow.
Then the point punched through with a squish
and he recoiled with a primitive howl that would
stay in her mind forever as the most chilling
sound she'd ever heard.

Reflexively he swung at her with the knife,
but she'd already slid out from under and was
rolling out of the closet and staggering to her
feet. The assailant lurched out after her, both
hands covering his face. His knife had dropped
to his feet and she saw it and wondered if she
could snatch it before he did. Her jab with the
wire hanger had penetrated one eye but he had
one good one left, and she knew that as long as
his heart beat at all he would come on, his determination as fixed as if his entire system had
been programmed with but one function: to
kill.

She circled out of range of his good eye, but
he stood almost atop the knife and she had to get

him off it. What she did next was either incredibly brave or incredibly stupid, and maybe it was a little of both. Picking up one of Mrs. Doyle's perfume atomizers, she threw it at him, shouting, "Over here! Over here, buddy!"

He pivoted in the direction of her voice, and as he did she pivoted with him so as to keep to his blind side. He staggered toward the spot she'd been in, giving her the opportunity to lunge for the knife. She grasped the handle with both hands. Suddenly all the agitation drained from her, and a calm and clarity settled upon her. "Over here, pal. Here I am. Come and get me," she beckoned, almost seductively.

If anyone had told her a mere three or four hours ago that she would be shoving a knife into a man's body she'd have had that person certified and committed to the funny farm. But now that she realized that this nightmare wasn't going to end by itself, that no one was going to shake her shoulder and say, "Come on, wake up, it's time to go to school," she felt capable of anything. She had, in the course of a half hour, gone from a wide-eyed innocent to a willing, even eager participant in this deadly game. No soldier had ever gone through a quicker basic training.

With one hand over his blind and bloody eye and the other swiping the air for a piece of his tormentress, he stumped toward her, bellowing in rage and pain. She crouched so that he loomed over her filling the space above with his black presence.

Now, Laurie?

No, not yet, one more second, let him get close enough to stumble over you.

Now, Laurie? Now, please? Hurry, before it's too late.

Yes. Now. Do it now, Laurie.

Just as his knees were about to collide with

her, she plunged the blade upward with both hands into his groin. The knife went in so easily she wasn't sure if she'd actually stabbed anything. Only his bellow of pure pain confirmed the strike. She wanted to twist and slash the blade inside his guts the way he'd done to Annie, but he dropped away from her, groaning, to a corner of the room, and she didn't want to risk administering a *coup de grace* in the dark.

The kids, meanwhile, were crying hysterically in the bathroom, and she had to get them out. She'd heard of people actually being frightened to death, and now she knew it was entirely possible. As it was, the kids would bear the mark of this traumatic night in their souls forevermore. And you, Laurie said to herself as she rushed to the bathroom door, won't do so badly in that department yourself.

It took her several minutes of pleading and reassuring to get them to open the door. She kept looking over her shoulder and listening. There was a stirring in the corner, but presently it ceased. He's *got* to be dead, she told herself. But her mind played back the memory of the big pickerel her daddy had caught on a trip he'd taken her on to the Wisconsin woods. Having forgotten to bring his creel, he wrapped the fish in newspaper and placed it in an old shopping bag. On the way home a half hour later, the fish, which she had thought long dead, began a violent death thrash that had startled both of them so much, her father had nearly driven into a tree.

At last she coaxed the children out of the bathroom. They fell blubbering into Laurie's arms. Their eyes were swollen from crying, and they trembled like puppies. "Listen to me, listen, children," she begged them. "Catch your breath. Breathe deeply, and don't think about it anymore. It's all over."

"You said that before."

"No, this time it really is all over. Now, I want you to walk to the door, down the stairs, and right out the front door."

"You're coming with us," Lindsey said, a question and a command.

"Listen to me. I want you to walk down the street to the MacKenzies and knock on their door. You tell them to call the police and send them over here. Do you understand?"

"Laurie, you come with us," Tommy pleaded.

"No! Do as I say."

She guided them across the bedroom to the head of the stairs and sent them off with a smack in the fanny each. They scampered downstairs and fled screaming into the night as Laurie collapsed on the top step to catch her breath and summon her wits for one last visit to the bedroom to make sure the monster was dead. She would never be able to sleep again if she did not witness for herself that it would never more raise a hand against mankind.

She buried her face in her hands and fought to regain control of herself.

Thus situated, she did not see the shadowy shape dragging itself out of the bedroom.

The shrieking came from the next block, and Loomis knew this was no Halloween prank. It was too late for children to be outside, and if that was not true terror in their cries for help, Loomis did not know what true terror was.

He cut across a lawn to find them racing up a walk to a white ranch house. They saw him, a Mephistophelean figure in goatee, bald head, and trench coat fluttering in the wind, and they shrieked even louder, turning tail and fleeing into a backyard. "It's him, the bogeyman!" he heard one shout.

He hurdled a rustic fence and dashed into the yard. "Children, it's all right," he murmured in his most reassuring tone, "it's all right, kids, I'm your friend."

They were not difficult to find. He spotted their light clothing behind a tree too narrow to conceal them, and though he knew it would scare the wits out of them if their wits hadn't been totally scared out of them already, he had to capture them to find out what they were running away from.

He tiptoed up to the tree, then dashed around it, tackling them both in strong but gentle arms. They broke into hysterical cries and wriggled in his arms in a desperate effort to escape. He clutched them tightly, uttering tender blandishments to soothe them until at last they relaxed long enough to answer his questions.

"Where are you coming from?"

"There," the little boy said with a general sweep of the western horizon.

"Where's there? Show me."

They escorted him back to the front lawn. Tommy pointed to a house catty-corner from their position. Its lights were out, its front door wide open.

"What's going on out there?" a voice shouted. A porch light went on and a man in pajamas stormed out of the house.

"There's trouble across the street. Serious trouble," Loomis said, dragging the children to the man by the collars of their shirts. "Take these kids and call the police at once. Get Sheriff Brackett. Tell him I've found our friend at . . . at that house there."

"The Doyle house?"

"Whichever that one is with the open door."

"Mister, this is no joke? I mean, I've been trick-or-treated to death tonight."

"You don't know what death is," Loomis hissed, drawing his gun as he rushed across the street.

Laurie inhaled deeply, realizing it was the first calm breath she'd taken since it all began. She lifted her face from her hands and contemplated the next move. She wasn't sure what it should be. She would have liked to wait for the police, but God knew if the kids had done what she'd instructed them to do. So she didn't want to wait. But she didn't want to flee the house either. Suppose she did and when she returned with the police he was gone. Would she ever sleep peacefully again, knowing he was out there, alive, lurking, stalking? No, she must either stand guard here outside the bedroom door, or . . .

. . . or go in there and look upon the still corpse, so that she could comfort herself with the image of his dead body whenever the horror visited her dreams.

That is, if he were dead.

Suppose he weren't?

She knew he was badly hurt. A needle in the neck, a hanger in the eye, a knife in the groin, surely no one who wasn't supernatural could endure such injuries and still live.

Then what held her back from going in there?

It was the realization that if by some miracle he *were* still alive, she would have to finish the job. She was no longer afraid that he could harm her; it was inconceivable to her that he could be *that* alive, let alone alive at all. No, it was the idea of actually murdering someone in cold blood. Self-defense was one thing. But a helpless man, even one who had slaughtered her three friends, who had attempted to do the same to her—well, she wasn't sure she could bring herself to do it.

Essentially she was not an avenger. Civilization was too deeply bred into her. The killer instinct had been diluted to the point where normally she could not imagine doing anything more harmful with a knife than cutting a slab of roast beef on her dinner plate.

The longer she sat the more confused and uncertain she became. She wished the decision could be taken out of her hands.

A moment later, it was.

In a night filled with startling horrors, this was the most startling and horrible of all, the hand on her hair, pulling at her scalp until she was sure he would tear it off her head like an orange peel. His other arm enclosed her throat, and only because she'd had her arms in front of her face did she prevent him from snapping her neck on the first blow.

As it was, she heard a bone snap in her wrist, and she knew it was all over this time. She'd been lucky three times, but she'd underestimated her foe. Now she was his. She kicked to her feet and squirmed in his grasp, hoping to kick them both down the stairs where he just might release her, but he guessed her strategy and yanked her away from the landing. His forearm tightened around the wrists pinned to her face, and the pain was so excruciating she knew she would pass out in another second.

Then she heard the explosion and felt his body jump as if someone had struck him with a fist. She was free. She fell to the floor. In her hand was a damp rubber mask. She looked for her assailant and found him leaning against a wall, a dark blotch spreading quickly over his right shoulder. Through the darkness and the flashing lights dancing in her eyes she looked at his face and saw it, white with whiter, fanglike teeth. His wet black hair was matted over his forehead, and one eye bulged like a dead fish's. Where his other eye had been was a wet bloody hole.

A movement on the stairs caught her attention. A bald man with a goatee was running up them, holding a huge black revolver with trembling hands. "Get out of the way!" he shouted at her.

She rolled away as he mounted the stairs. The dying man staggered into the bedroom toward the French windows that opened on the Doyles' sun deck. The bald man reached the landing and stepped into the bedroom, leveling his gun at the retreating figure.

The explosions were ear-splitting. Laurie was deafened by the first and felt rather than heard the subsequent ones. She saw the assailant lurch back with each gunshot as if struck with a bat. He crashed backward through the French windows and tumbled from the sun deck into the backyard below. The moon and street light caught the blood-gloss of at least three bullet holes in his chest.

She did not ask at first who her rescuer was. She simply fell into his arms and burst into wracking sobs. His embrace was so comforting she could have fallen asleep in it. Maybe, if she did, she would wake up to find the world as it had been this morning. This morning? Was it a mere sixteen or seventeen hours since she had stood on her doorstep bantering with her father? It seemed as if she'd lived three lifetimes in that scant time.

Suddenly she was in pain. The adrenaline that seemed to act as an anaesthetic started to wear off. Her ankle throbbed where she'd twisted it dropping over the stairs at Lindsey's house. Her wrist ached and had begun to swell where he'd cracked the bone. Her slashed arm tingled agonizingly. Her scalp felt as if someone had taken a tomahawk to it. No, these were not the symptoms of a dream. This was the nightmare of reality. It would take her years to absorb this truth, and a lifetime to ponder it.

The man released her, and she looked up at him. "Thank you. Are you a policeman?"

He smiled. "No, just a friend."

"A friend with a gun, thank God."

"Thank God." Loomis was trembling. He hyperventilated several times to slow down his racing heart. Then he walked to the shattered windows and peered down.

It lay on its back amid a thousand shards of broken glass that twinkled in the moonlight like hoarfrost. The front of the uniform stolen from the truck driver glistened blackly with blood that seeped out of the tremendous rents in his flesh caused by Loomis's magnum. One of its eyes gazed stupidly up to the sky; where the other had been was a black hole caked with clotted blood and jellied aqueous humor. Loomis stared at the corpse a long time, watching for a sign of life. Detecting none, he turned back into the bedroom and reached into his trench coat pocket.

"What are you doing?" the girl asked.

"Reloading," he said, pushing the long heavy cartridges into the chamber of his gun.

"Why?"

Loomis shrugged. "It heightens my sense of security," he said with an irony that was lost on her. He started down the steps.

"Where are you going?"

"To examine the body. I would like you to go across the street and wait for the police."

"No," said Laurie. "I think I'd like to come with you."

Loomis looked at her quizzically. "You haven't had enough for one night?"

"I want to make sure it's all over."

"Suit yourself. I assure you it is."

Which is why you're reloading your gun,

Loomis said to himself, heading downstairs. From the way the girl clutched his arm he knew she was thinking the same thing. Poor child. If she knew what he knew, she'd be thinking darker thoughts than that even.

She'd be thinking about the dream that little Michael, angelic choirboy face turned to the ceiling as if in prayer, had told him some fifteen years ago, a dream about his vengeance on a Druid girl who had not returned his love, and on her lover who had mocked him, a dream about a ceremony on an accursed gravesite, where his head and heart were left exposed to the elements to rot while some shaman recited an awful curse dooming him to roam the earth forever lusting for blood.

She'd be thinking about Michael's great-grandfather, who had been tortured by that identical dream, a dream that had inflamed both of them to commit deeds of wanton horror.

She'd be thinking about the voices that spoke both to Michael and to his great-grandfather, urging them to take revenge against someone who had lived over a thousand years ago.

She'd be thinking about a festival called Samhain, whose grotesque rituals designed to protect Druid harvests against the depredations of howling demons had been transformed over a millennium or more into the harmless holiday called Halloween.

Halloween. Charming children in cute costumes begging sweets, cardboard cutouts of skeletons and witches on brooms, warmly glowing jack-o'-lanterns, artless parties and entertaining games, spooky movies on TV, innocent pranks, trick-or-treat.

Loomis exited into the cool night air and rounded the side of the house, trailed by Laurie. Cautiously, he prowled toward the backyard, the moonlight glinting on the blue barrel of his gun.

One more corner to turn. Loomis stuck his head slowly around it and focused his eyes on the place where the body had landed beneath the French windows.

It was gone.

He rushed to the spot, suppressing a sob of frustration. A patch of flattened grass surrounded by twinkling shards of glass. No other sign, not even blood.

Above the thudding of his heart he heard the girl whimper behind him. He turned and put his hand under her arm to support her. Mutely they stared at the patch of grass.

Until this moment he had hoped against hope that the entity he had pursued to this place was a thing of flesh and blood like himself, though deep in his heart he had known it would be otherwise. The evidence pointed not merely to another interpretation but, as he had said to Sheriff Brackett, to another dimension.

He shuddered, wondering what little boy at this very moment was tossing in his sleep, tortured by a dream of tragic love that had occurred far away and long ago, tormented by a voice commanding the dreamer to take revenge.

Laurie's nails dug into his shoulder as she stared like a soldier in shell shock at the empty place on the lawn. "It *was* the bogeyman, wasn't it?" she murmured.

"As a matter of fact," Loomis replied, "it was."

RELAX!
SIT DOWN
and Catch Up On Your Reading!

THE LATEST BOOKS
IN THE BANTAM
BESTSELLING TRADITION

☐	12998	**THE FAR PAVILIONS** M. M. Kaye	$3.
☐	13752	**SHADOW OF THE MOON** M. M. Kaye	$3.
☐	13545	**SOPHIE'S CHOICE** William Styron	$3.
☐	14115	**INDEPENDENCE!** Dana Fuller Ross	$2.
☐	14070	**NEBRASKA!** Dana Fuller Ross	$2.
☐	14325	**WYOMING!** Dana Fuller Ross	$2.
☐	14045	**WHITE INDIAN** Donald Clayton Porter	$2.
☐	13559	**THE RENEGADE** Donald Clayton Porter	$2.
☐	13452	**THE HAWK AND THE DOVE** Leigh Franklin James	$2.
☐	12271	**LOVESWEPT** Lynn Lowery	$2.
☐	12961	**LARISSA** Lynn Lowery	$2.
☐	12958	**THE CINNAMON GARDENS** Jeanette Rebuth	$2.
☐	14026	**A WORLD FULL OF STRANGERS** Cynthia Freeman	$2.
☐	13641	**PORTRAITS** Cynthia Freeman	$3.
☐	13463	**BLUE ROSES** Joyce Selznick	$2.
☐	14064	**DAYS OF WINTER** Cynthia Freeman	$2.
☐	14063	**FAIRYTALES** Cynthia Freeman	$2.
☐	14033	**ICE!** Arnold Federbush	$2.
☐	11820	**FIREFOX** Craig Thomas	$2.